MISS SPELLED

MORGANA BEST

Miss Spelled

(The Kitchen Witch, Book 1)

Copyright © 2015 by Morgana Best

ISBN 978-1-925674-14-9

By this act
And words of rhyme
Trouble not
These books of mine
With these words I now thee render
Candle burn and bad return
3 times stronger to its sender.
(Ancient Celtic)

GLOSSARY

The author has used Australian spelling in this series, so for example, *Mum* instead of the US spelling *Mom*, *neighbour* instead of the US spelling *neighbor*, *realise* instead of the US spelling *realize*. It is *Ms*, *Mr* and *Mrs* in Australia, not *Ms.*, *Mr.* and *Mrs.*; *cosy* and not *cozy*; *1930s* not *1930's*; *offence* not *offense*; *centre* not *center*; *towards* not *toward*; *jewellery* not *jewelry*; *favour* not *favor*; *mould* not *mold*; *two storey house* not *two story house*; *practise* (verb) not *practice* (verb); *odour* not *odor*; *smelt* not *smelled*; *travelling* not *traveling*; *liquorice* not *licorice*; *leant* not *leaned*; *have concussion* not *have a concussion*; *anti clockwise* not *counterclockwise*; *go to hospital* not *go to the hospital*; *sceptic* not *skeptic*; *aluminium* not *aluminum*; *learnt* not *learned*. These are just some of the differences.

Please note that these are not mistakes or typos, but correct Aussie spelling and terms.

AUSTRALIAN SLANG AND TERMS

Big Smoke - a city

Blighter - infuriating or good-for-nothing person

Blimey - an expression of surprise

Blue - an argument

Bluestone - copper sulphate (copper sulfate in US spelling)

Bluo - a blue laundry additive, an optical brightener

Boot (car) - trunk (car)

Bonnet (car) - hood (car)

Bunging it on - faking something, pretending

Cark it - die

Come good - turn out okay

Copper, cop - police officer

Coot - silly or annoying person

Drongo - an idiot

Dunny - an outhouse, a toilet, often ramshackle

Fair crack of the whip - a request to be fair, reasonable, just

Flat out like a lizard drinking water - very busy

Galah - an idiot

Garbage - trash

G'day - Hello

Give a lift (to someone) - give a ride (to someone)

Goosebumps - goose pimples

Laundry (referring to the room) - laundry room

Like a stunned mullet - very surprised

Mad as a cut snake - either insane or very angry

Miles - while Australians have kilometres these days, it is common to use expressions such as, "The road stretched for miles," "It was miles away."

Mow (grass / lawn) - cut (grass / lawn)

Stone the crows! - an expression of surprise

Takeaway (food) - Take Out (food)

Torch - flashlight

Tuck in (to food) - to eat food hungrily

Ute /Utility - pickup truck

Vegemite - Australian food spread, thick, dark brown

Wardrobe - closet

Indigenous References

Bush tucker - food that occurs in the Australian bush

Koori - the original inhabitants/traditional custodians of the land of Australia in the part of NSW in which this book is set. *Murri* are the people just to the north. White European culture often uses the term, *Aboriginal people*.

I hugged the blue hippo I'd snagged at the hospital gift shop as I made my way through the sterile halls of the patient wing. I hated hospitals. In fact, I could count on one hand all the times I had ever stepped foot in one voluntarily. Nothing good ever came from having to come to a hospital.

I was being silly, of course. I knew that Brad was safe and sound. Why he had to remain in the hospital at all was a mystery to me. He hadn't even returned my calls. He had only sent me a text sometime in the early hours of the morning, a text that read 'Food poisoning!' followed by several exclamation marks.

I could only assume that Brad was overreacting, given his tendency to do so. He was handsome. In fact, he was downright gorgeous. He was the manager at a local men's clothing store, and had even modelled for website pictures for the store's clothing line. The problem was that Brad could be overly dramatic. A simple cold needed bed rest. A lost bowling match was rigged by the other team. He got himself uninvited to poker night with some of his male friends, whom he deemed elitists and other words I could not repeat.

It was hard to believe that someone like Brad would want to date a Plain Jane like I was. I wasn't exactly a super model. I have dark brown hair, hazel eyes, and an unremarkable body. And yet for some reason, he'd had eyes for me ever since we had met at a party. He had a charming smile, and always seemed to know what he wanted.

Brad had even encouraged me to learn to cook. I wasn't much into cooking. I was always busy, so it was simpler to buy food and warm it in the microwave. In fact, if the package didn't have microwave instructions, then it didn't even make my shopping cart in the first place. It just didn't make sense to spend time over a stove, especially if I could make it in five minutes and not even have to stay in the kitchen. Besides, my attempts at cooking had proven fruitless at best. What's more, I usually set something on fire.

I frowned and squeezed the defenceless stuffed animal as I studied the room numbers. Home cooking couldn't be all that great if it could land someone in the hospital, I figured. Even if it was just an upset stomach, it was hard to think of Brad in one of these places. Surely he didn't get stuck in this place over last night's nachos? Perhaps he ate something after he left my house? I know I hadn't cooked the chicken for long, but I thought that was a good idea at the time, to save the smoke alarms going off again. I'd been pleased that it wasn't another charcoal dinner.

I shook my head and smiled to myself. The fact that Brad had been considerate enough not to bother me at work was proof that he knew he'd be fine. It was wonderfully kind of him not to insist on me staying at his side, as he knew how much I disliked hospitals.

Finally. I sighed as I saw the room number and Brad's name. I politely knocked on the door and then made my way in. "Hi, Brad. How are you doing?" I beamed at him, but my smile faded when he shot me a scathing look.

"What are you doing here?" he demanded.

I looked at his mobile phone lying beside him. He was apparently keeping an eye on it, so he had, in fact, seen my messages. Why hadn't he responded?

His lips curled into a sneer. "I knew you were thick, but are you really stupid enough not to know when you aren't wanted?"

My jaw fell as I stared at him in confusion. Where in the world did that come from? Was it his medication making him act this way?

"You are really something, aren't you?" Brad threw the blue hippo onto the floor. "You almost killed me, you stupid cow!"

I blinked, struck mute with shock. Somewhere in the back of my mind, I knew I needed to let him have it. I knew I should not let a man talk to me that way, but my mind was a complete blank. Brad had never talked to me that way. He had never called me stupid, or a cow. Tears welled in my eyes as I struggled to control myself.

This only seemed to make him all the more agitated. "Oh, don't act like you're some innocent victim! You put me in a hospital. I knew you were never going to be a five star chef, but how hard is it to make a bowl of nachos without having to call an ambulance?"

"Brad, I ate them too, and I'm not sick," I pointed out in desperation. I had never seen this side of him. What in the world was going on?

"Yeah, *you* didn't get sick. Just get out of here," he said, as he leant back against his pillow. "We're done."

"Done?" I whispered.

"Done. Over. *Finito*," he said in a slow, mocking tone. "I only dated you because you're so plain and desperate that I figured I wouldn't have to worry about you getting picked up by other men. I don't need an ugly woman who doesn't know how to cook or even do laundry. What good are you?"

My mind couldn't begin to process what I had just heard. I blinked at him as I tried to find the words to say. I wanted to tell him off, call him names, say something witty, anything! Yet my mind was a complete blank.

I couldn't remember precisely how events unfolded after that. I had a dim memory of pouring a pitcher of water over him during his tirade about the time he had wasted with me. I was still reeling over it. How in the world did nachos end our relationship? It wasn't real, was it?

Looking back, I felt like an idiot. There were so many small warning signs, little signs so easy to ignore. I never once imagined that I would have fallen for such an awful jerk. Weren't women supposed to have some sort of radar against that sort of thing? People acted as if seeing the signs was easy.

I wiped my eyes and took a deep breath as I made my way back to work. I just wanted to get through today, and then spend the weekend hiding in my apartment with bags of jelly beans, a huge amount of ice cream, and old movies. Was there a minimum age limit for becoming one of those crazy cat ladies? Cats seemed to be so much better company at the moment. The only problem was that my apartment building did not allow pets.

I was a little relieved that there was a big meeting that afternoon. I didn't know the specifics, only that the higher-ups were making an announcement. That would take my mind off my upsetting break-up with Brad, and I was hopeful it was good news.

Several employees had been pushing for a raise in benefits for the Complaints Department. They were requesting more full-time positions for the ones with high satisfaction ratings, which was a requirement to receive a company health plan. They were also petitioning for a pay raise across the board, to compensate for having to deal with the cursing, insults, threats and other ugly aspects of human behaviour. In the Complaints Department, my colleagues and I spent hours being blamed for the customer's misery.

Perhaps my day would improve and I would get a pay raise. I still needed to pay for a new oven, the repainted ceilings, and the lingering smell of charred fish in my apartment. Last week's fried fish dinner had been a disaster. My landlord had been far from pleased, and my timing couldn't have been worse. It happened right after I was three days late getting in my rent.

I hurried to take a seat at the back, so I could finish composing myself while I was in the meeting. Hopefully, the big announcement today would put everybody in such a good mood that the afternoon of angry and inconvenienced callers would fly by. I needed a good distraction from Brad.

As soon as the meeting began, my hopes for good news were quickly dashed. The management seemed awfully grim, and the heads of the Complaints Department looked miserable, nothing at all like people who had just won pay rises for their department. And even stranger, the high up managers were observing as well. They never came to the Complaints Department.

My stomach clenched with anxiety when one of the managers stepped forward and addressed the crowd. I wasn't the only apprehensive one. There were nervous whispers all around me.

"I will keep this brief," the man began. He was wearing a too-tight suit and a bland expression on his face. His voice was monotone. He could easily have been a robot. "As you all know, there has been much discussion regarding the human resources of the Complaints Department. However, the ongoing debate over benefits and hours has been tabled due to a significant shift in structure."

The man paused, and we all looked at each other. He cleared his throat and looked around the room. "The Complaints Department is being outsourced to an offshore company in India, effective immediately. Please clear your desks this afternoon. Payments owed, including those in lieu of notice, will be mailed to your current addresses."

Just like that, twenty people were without a job. He could have been commenting on the weather, or the colour of someone's shirt. The man continued speaking, but to me, his voice was nothing but a blur. I was fired? The man did not look the slightest bit sorry that the higher-ups had thrown our jobs overseas.

There was an uproar from the other employees as they frantically tried to argue and protest the sudden announcement. I simply turned and went to my cubicle to decide what I needed to take home with me.

I had lost my boyfriend and my job in the same day. What were the odds? At least things couldn't get any worse.

CHAPTER 2

I wiped my eyes once again as I forced one foot in front of the other. It had been a long time since I had made it home so early in the day. I had bought jelly beans, ice cream, and a sales bin movie on my way home. I was going to get a long, hot bath, pop something in the microwave, and drown my sorrows in empty calories and a collection of old black and white romantic comedies. Nothing beats the classics.

Tomorrow I would talk to the landlord about an extension, and fire up my résumé on every online job site known to humankind. If I was lucky, I would land something quickly. It didn't have to be a great job; it just had to keep a roof over my head and the lights on.

I reached my apartment with a sigh of relief,

glad to be done with the awful day. I rummaged for my keys and thought with a laugh that with Brad gone, at least I could promise the landlord my cooking days were over.

That was when I glanced down and saw the corner of an envelope sticking out from under the door. I bent over and carefully pried it out so I didn't rip it. With the way my luck was running, I would have mangled it just opening the door to get to it. My heart sank when I recognised the landlord's handwriting.

I unlocked my door with shaking hands, flung it open, and then rushed inside, eager to open the letter and see how bad it was. I threw my bag onto a table, and opened the envelope. It was no doubt the bill for painting the ceilings in the hallway outside my apartment after the smoke damage, and I fervently hoped it wasn't a large bill.

I ripped open the envelope and read the letter. It was not a bill. I read it the second time, and then the third, but that didn't change the contents of the letter, no matter how badly I willed it so.

'You have fourteen days from this date to vacate the premises. The reasons include fire hazards, property damage, and repeated complaints by tenants about smoke emanating from your apartment.'

I sank to the floor, the letter in my hands. I could no longer see the letter; my vision was blurred by hot tears. I tried to take a calming breath, but I didn't have any more calm to spare. I crumpled the paper in my hands and threw it at the door with a cry of frustration.

Why?

Everything was gone, all in one day. I had no home. No job. Not even a boyfriend to lean on.

Everything had been taken from me. All in one ugly day. Was it karma? Had I done something wrong? Was this some sort of punishment?

As I sobbed, I tried in vain to find a silver lining. Usually, I was a super optimist and could always manage to find a silver lining in anything. But what did I have?

I was alone. My parents had died when I was fourteen, and I had been passed from one resentful relative to another. Given how much they disliked taking care of me when I was an obligation, I very much doubted that they would allow me a month or two to get back on my feet.

I thought of the cramped and dirty experience I'd had at the shelters when I turned seventeen and managed to become emancipated. I shuddered and felt a whimper escape my lips. I couldn't go back to shelters and project housing. I just couldn't.

I curled up until my forehead touched my knees, and I wept. As my wails grew louder, I planted my hands over my mouth so other residents wouldn't hear me. *Now remember, no matter how hard things get, it won't be anything you can't handle.* Dad always used to say that to me, back when I was a teenager and when everything was the end of the world. All these years later, I could still remember the way his eyes would crinkle when he was trying to assure me that the world would not end because I wore a second hand uniform.

How petty those problems seemed after the accident that took my parents away from me.

I didn't know how long I sat sobbing on the floor. I thought it was all too much to bear, and then I regretted that last thought. No, that wasn't right to say. It could be worse. I remembered the foggy cemetery, the twin headstones, and the sound of dirt as it hit the pine wood boxes. It could be so much worse.

I straightened myself up and wiped my eyes as I sniffled and stretched out my sore joints. I didn't have any time for a pity party. I needed to clean up and get ready to deal with these problems. I still had an hour or two before the unemployment office closed. I needed to register for benefits as soon as possible.

I wiped my nose and made a mental list of things I needed to do. I couldn't afford a mover. And unless I found a job fast, I had no proof of income or a deposit for another apartment. The landlord sure wasn't going to give me a reference.

I was going to have to resign myself to the idea that I could only save the belongings that could fit into the back of my car. If only my car was a mini-van! As it was, I wouldn't be able to fit much into it. I had been thinking of the environment and gas mileage when I'd bought it, not about moving my belongings in an emergency. Thank goodness the car was paid off. If my car had been taken from me when I didn't have a roof over my head—yes, things could actually be much worse.

I grimaced and started towards the door to reclaim the crumpled paper. There was probably a place I needed to sign and return it to the office. The landlord was compulsive when it came to paperwork. I had better get that done before anything else.

My eyes fell on a second, undamaged envelope on the floor just in front of the door. I cringed, and a wave of nausea hit me. That was probably the massive repair bill, just to add insult to injury. Tears sprang to my eyes again as I bent down to pick it up.

I at once saw that the letter was not addressed in the landlord's harsh, blocky handwriting. I turned it over, and written in flowery handwriting was the name, 'Ruprecht Foxtin-Flynn.'

It must be someone suing me. Surely only a high paid lawyer would have a name like Ruprecht Foxtin-Flynn. I was exasperated as I ripped open the envelope. Who in the world would be suing me? One of the neighbours?

I unfolded the paper. I didn't have the energy to be surprised that it started with the words, 'I regret to inform you.' No, that was pretty much in line with my whole day.

I stopped reading and went to get a soda and open the packet of jelly beans. If I was going to get slammed with more bad news, I was going to be sitting with my comfort foods first.

I bit into a yellow jelly bean and tried to savour it as I studied the return address on the back of the envelope. It looked official. Whoever was regretting to inform me of something, appeared to be someone important.

I shoved some more jelly beans into my mouth, and unfolded the letter once more. Might as well rip off the band-aid fast and deal with the pain all at once, right?

Dear Ms Amelia Spelled,

I regret to inform you that your aunt, Ms Angelica Spelled, has crossed over to the other side. I am the designated executor of her will. At your convenience, I require an audience with you to finalise your inheritance. Please see the included documents as to the details of your inheritance and my contact information.

With very best wishes.

Yours truly,

Ruprecht Foxtin-Flynn.

I reread the letter and tried to remember my aunt. I felt bad that I could not remember anything to bring a sense of loss. My father had a sister, but I couldn't remember her. Had I ever seen her? *Angelica Spelled.* Mum and Dad said something about me having an aunt who was highly eccentric, but I don't remember them mentioning her name. They had told me that they cut ties with her a long time ago, but they had never told why they had done so.

I wondered why an estranged relative was leaving me something in her will. The only relatives I had experienced had resented me. There had been no mistaking their dislike for having to care for an extra child, especially when they did all they could to push me off onto the others.

I flipped the page. It looked fairly standard. Family photos were listed. Okay, that was good. I had always wanted to make an album. If I was lucky, there would be pictures of my parents when they were younger. Next on the list was bone china. That was going to be harder to deal with. I could hardly live in my car with bone china. Hopefully, it was antique, and I could sell it. Then I read the next item that I had inherited.

All remaining property, including house, contents, and store.

I read it about five times, waiting for it to disappear and be something like a doll house and not a real house—but it was a real house. And a store? My aunt had left me a store: an income-producing store?

I read everything carefully. Was I dreaming? There was no way. There was no way that I'd lost my home, job, and relationship, and then inherited a house and my own business, all in less than a day.

I stared at the hand-written phone number on the corner of the envelope and rubbed my chin. No, it couldn't be real, right? This was the part where I called and Ruprecht Foxtin-Flynn would turn out be a con man trying to get me to send money to an overseas address, or he'd ask for my credit card number for 'processing fees.' I, Amelia Spelled, was not that person who got an inheritance from a mysterious relative.

I chewed on my bottom lip thoughtfully and checked the time. Then, I reached for my mobile phone.

CHAPTER 3

I was ready to get out of the car by the time I finally crossed the town border and found myself in Bayberry Creek. The charming little town sprang up out of nowhere, various homes appearing first, and then some businesses and one small school lined the road. As I continued on to the centre of town, my GPS went haywire, the screen blinking nothing but green and black for a few moments. When it came back on, the streets were gone, but the blue line remained, and it showed me that I should be turning right.

I did so at the next intersection, and I continued on awhile, away from the main hub that was the middle of town and towards more houses. One house in particular caught my attention, a pretty grey and white home surrounded by a lush green lawn and magnolia trees. The home was Victorian, with beautiful antique iron lacework along the front veranda and a black iron gate. I almost drove off the road due to looking at the home so much. Somehow it reminded me of something, but try as I might, I couldn't get my brain to focus long enough to come up with what it was.

Then I was past the house and the memory remained hidden, while I had to deal with my GPS malfunctioning one more time. It flashed green and black again, but now when it stopped, the streets were back along with the blue line. It was telling me that I had gone too far. I wondered how that could be. I slowed my car and made a U-turn as soon as there was break in the light traffic.

The GPS led me to a small shop on the corner of two streets with bird names, Crow Lane and Raven Street. The building was made of red bricks which had faded to a dusky pink after long years under the sun. The front of the store was mostly glass, and I could see inside it as I parked alongside the curb. The store looked to be a book store, although there were some antique pieces in the window. The sign hanging over the doorway on a small black chain swaying softly in the wind simply read, *Glinda's*.

I climbed out of my car and took some time to stretch my legs. I stretched my arms over my head and bent backwards, groaning a little as I heard some cracks. I had never been one for long car rides.

My car was crammed full of luggage, just about everything I owned, and it had been hard to see out of my back window since a stack of folded blankets obstructed most of the glass.

As I walked to the front door of the store, it swung open suddenly. A man appeared there. I hadn't seen him coming, even though the door was mostly glass, apart from a metal bar bisecting it in the middle. The man was slim and elderly, his head mostly bald save a few wisps of white hair which curled wildly this way and that. His skin was pale and thin looking, spotted brown in places. He looked like a wizard from *Harry Potter* or *Lord of the Rings*.

He must have seen the startled expression on my face, because he smiled sheepishly and extended his hand. "Did I scare you?" he asked.

"Oh no, no," I said hurriedly. "I wasn't paying attention." Well, I was pretty sure I had been paying plenty of attention.

The man laughed and held the door open for me. "Come in, come in. I'm betting you're Amelia."

I nodded as I stepped into the shop. It seemed like the kind of place in which I could spend a lot of time, and I had only seen a fraction of it. There were rows and rows of books on shelves that were no more than three or four feet high. There were also numerous antiques. It dawned on me that this was both a bookstore and an antique store. I supposed this was common in a small country town like this one. "And you're Ruprecht?" I felt silly as soon as I said it. I mean, who else could he be? Dumbledore?

"Please call me Ruprecht," the man said with another grin. His smiles were warm and freely given. I didn't know the man, but I liked him already.

"And *Glinda's*, like the good witch," I said.

Ruprecht tilted his head to the side and raised one of his bushy grey eyebrows. "Come again?"

"Glinda, the good witch. From *The Wizard of Oz*?"

"Oh, never seen it," Ruprecht said, shaking his head. He lifted his hands and let them fall in a dismissive manner, as though he had more important things to do than watch one of the most popular and beloved films of all time.

"Oh well, never mind then," I said with a laugh. "I love your store."

"You've barely seen it," he said. "Take a peek as we head into the back. I've just brewed some tea, if you'd like."

I am more of a coffee person, but I could sit through a cup of tea for the sake of being polite. Ruprecht turned and hurried towards the back of the store, leaving me to follow along behind. I turned my head this way and that as I tried to take in as much of the shop as I could. It was something of a labyrinth.

The back room was cramped, with a small sink in the corner and a counter next to it. There was a tiny stove with only two burners, on one of which sat a blue kettle that looked to be made of tin, and was maybe as old as Ruprecht, if not older. He picked up the kettle and poured tea into two small, thick white cups. When he handed me my cup, I was surprised to realise that the cup was made of bone. Surely I was wrong, but when I pulled the rim of the cup to my lips, I hesitated just a moment before I allowed my mouth to touch it.

"I can take you to your aunt's house tomorrow,

after the funeral service which I mentioned to you on the phone. I'm afraid the house isn't quite ready for you, so I took the liberty of booking you into a hotel tonight. It's a nice little place out on the edge of town," Ruprecht said.

"Oh, thank you," I said, wondering what he meant about the house not being ready.

Ruprecht must have read my mind, or else he simply knew I would be wondering such a thing, because he smiled and waved his hand through the air. "Not to worry, dear, just cleaning a few things up, making a few small repairs, things like that. Cleaning out the gutters, so to speak. I took care of it all. I didn't want you to have a thing to worry about at this trying time. I know it must be hard to lose a family member."

I didn't feel the need to mention that I didn't know anything about my Aunt Angelica beyond the fact that my parents had told me that she was extremely odd. I don't remember ever meeting her. Instead, I nodded sombrely and took another sip of tea. As I was trying to think of something to say, I heard a soft meowing. I turned towards the door which led to the store proper, and there was a cat, fat and orange with a white streak running down the centre of its face. It was joined by another cat, this one black, and much slimmer. Both cats sat in the doorway, their little heads tilted upwards as their eyes remained on me. It made me uncomfortable. It was as if they were staring right through me.

"How long have you had this place?" I asked as I turned from the cats to look at Ruprecht once more.

He took a moment to finish his tea before answering. "A lifetime," he said, and then he set his cup down next to the sink. "I can give you the tour."

"Thanks, I'd love that," I said. I finished my own cup and set it next to Ruprecht's.

He led me out into the shop. The cats ran in front of him and then disappeared beneath a heavy oak writing desk that looked as old as the hills.

We spent half an hour or so going through the shop, Ruprecht pointing out his favourite pieces as we looked at the antique furniture and knick knacks. It was a strange sort of shop, with an almost arcane feel to it. The sky outside was growing dark when we paused by the front door.

"I can give you directions to the hotel, and they have a key waiting for you at the front desk."

I smiled. "Thanks so much."

"Tomorrow I'll introduce you to Thyme, who

was your aunt's assistant at the shop," Ruprecht said.

"I don't even know what kind of shop it is," I said, shaking my head. "I hadn't seen my aunt in a long time, if ever," I finally admitted, "and this has all happened so fast."

Ruprecht nodded his head. "Well, dear, it's one of my favourite places in town. It's a cake shop, to be precise."

My mouth fell open. A cake shop? What did I know about baking? Hadn't my terrible cooking just gotten me evicted? Hadn't it cost me my boyfriend, a man I had thought I would marry? I couldn't run a cake store, any more than the elderly man in front of me could run a marathon. I forced my face to twist into some sort of look which hopefully could be mistaken for delight, but inside I was worried, and frankly, crushed. Why couldn't my aunt have owned this bookstore? Or just about any other business?

I had, of course, wondered what sort of store it was from the time I had received the letter until I arrived in Bayberry Creek, but I hadn't worried too much. I had just counted my blessings that I owned a business, any business at all. It was better than being homeless and penniless.

"She's left all of her recipes with Thyme," Ruprecht went on. He appeared to be oblivious to my distress. "So I'm sure you can step in, and we people here in town won't have to go long without your aunt's famous chocolate cream cupcakes."

I smiled, a smile that betrayed my feelings of horror and utter despair. "I'll do my best," I said.

CHAPTER 4

The next morning I awoke with a stiff back, the price I paid for spending hours in the car the day before. I took a long, hot shower, letting the steaming water pound on my back and work out the kinks for me. As I was drying my hair using the hotel hair dryer that could not be unplugged from the wall, the small white phone in the other room rang. I was startled. On the one hand, I hadn't anticipated any calls. I didn't think anyone would know I was here, and on the other hand, I associated the sound of the landline ringing with people chasing me to pay overdue bills.

I rushed from the bathroom in a white terry cloth robe, although of course, the other person on the phone wouldn't be able to see me. I smiled when I heard Ruprecht's voice.

"Amelia, I wanted to ask you to come to a small get together this morning. It's before the funeral proper, just some of your aunt's best friends and most loved companions getting together."

I thought that sounded nice, so I jotted down directions on the small pad of paper that was kept next to the phone and told him I would be there. When I hung up, I finished drying my hair, and then dressed.

I had left my car mostly packed the night before, only taking out one of the suitcases. It was a funeral, so black was in order, and I thought I looked pretty good in a black skirt which fell to my ankles and a modest black top. It felt strange to feel good about myself as I looked in the mirror, since I was going to a funeral after all, but I had been a mess since my break up. It was nice to feel as though I had some worth, if even only in such a shallow way as looking nice.

I followed the directions I had written down as I slowly drove through town. There was a stretch of bushland that ran along the southern part of Bayberry Creek, and that was where the directions led. I parked in a small lot with a few other cars, and had been instructed to follow a dirt path there into the bushland. I had walked only a couple of hundred yards before I saw Ruprecht. He was wearing a suit, all black except for the white shirt, and his tie had small red dots upon a yellow field. He took my hand warmly, and then motioned for me to step off the path. "Walk right down there, to the edge of the creek," he said. "You can't miss it."

And indeed I wouldn't have been able to miss it, because I was one of the last to arrive. There was a small group of people here, all of them women, most of them older. A massive iron pot sat near the water, and it appeared to be filled with dirt. Next to it, on a small table which seemed out of place in the bushland, was a bowl of seeds. To the left of that was a large circle made of flowers lying on the ground. The wind was strong here between the trees, and the flowers swayed this way and that, but surprisingly they didn't scatter into the wind, which would have taken them right out to the clear water in the small stream.

"Amelia, this is my granddaughter, Mint," Ruprecht called from behind me.

When I turned, I saw a young woman who was near my own age standing next to the old man. I smiled and shook her hand. Mint was wearing all black, and her hair was as black as night. She had bracelets all up her right arm, starting at the wrist and going almost up to her elbow. They all appeared to be made of hemp, and they all had a single glossy stone tied among them somewhere.

"Nice to meet you," Mint said. "I'm sorry about your aunt. We all loved her very much."

I nodded. I felt bad that I wasn't too distraught about my aunt's death, simply because I hadn't known her. I also felt bad as I didn't know whether I should tell Mint this.

"Camino is an ancient historian of sorts, and a classical scholar," Ruprecht said from behind me, making me jump. "In fact, she's your new next-door neighbour."

I swung around to see an elderly woman in a white, flowing floor-length dress. I smiled and shook her extended hand, keeping one eye on Ruprecht, who was heading for the centre of the flower ring, making sure to step over the flowers and not disturb them. He was opening his mouth to speak when he stopped and looked pointedly towards the tree line from the small clearing we stood in. I saw a woman, more or less my own age, hurrying into the clearing, wearing a bright yellow dress and an easy smile.

"I'm Thyme," she said to me. "I keep everything running at the shop," she added with a laugh.

"We're going to begin now," Ruprecht said, and Thyme fell quiet. As Ruprecht began, I turned and looked at everyone in the clearing. There were only ten or so people here. I wondered if there would be more at the funeral proper in a couple of hours.

Ruprecht spoke of Angelica, and he spoke fondly. He didn't speak for long before he was stepping out of the flowers. "Would anyone like to say anything?" he asked, and Thyme was the first one to go forward and take Ruprecht's place within the circle.

"Angelica was more than just an employer to me, and even more than just a friend. She was like a mother. As to you she was like family. It's never easy to lose family, but we, more than anyone else, know that death is just the beginning of a great journey. We can take solace in knowing that Angelica's spirit exists and carries on. She was many things, most of all though, she was a friend."

I thought Thyme had finished speaking, but she went on. "I remember the first cake of Angelica's I tried. My goodness. That's all I have to say, right?" There were some nods and laughter throughout the group. "What a talent the woman had. What a talent, and I'll miss her."

More nodding, and then Thyme was done. A few other women spoke, and I realised that Ruprecht was the only man there. After they had finished speaking, everyone looked at me as if they expected me to speak, but I had been moved to tears by the kind words everyone had been saying about the aunt I didn't know. It was powerful, unlike anything I had ever felt. I managed to get out of speaking with some grace, probably due to my tears. Thyme even came over and rubbed my back softly as Ruprecht went back to the circle.

"Please, let's gather by the basin and each plant a seed. Remember our friend as we do so."

A line quickly formed at the iron pot, and I went as well. I had never seen anything like it, but one by one the women picked up a seed and pressed it into the earth that sat in the pot. When it was my turn, I took a seed and placed it on the dirt, pausing a moment before using the tip of my index finger to press it down. I found myself wishing once again that I had known my aunt.

Everyone spent an hour or so mingling by the creek, and I was introduced to the other women, although I spent most of my time speaking to

Ruprecht, his granddaughter, Mint, as well as Thyme.

We all then headed for my aunt's grave, and apparently so did what looked like the rest of the town. There were so many mourners here that I thought there was a good chance the whole town had come. Angelica must have been a pretty good baker.

Ruprecht presided over this as well. He gave another beautiful speech, and afterwards Angelica's casket was lowered into a hole in the ground. Everyone took a handful of dirt and tossed it onto the shining wood.

Ruprecht introduced me to more people when the ceremony was over. They all hugged me and told me how sorry they were for my loss, and how nice it was to meet me.

The only person I didn't like was a man named Brant McCallum. He was slimy looking, in a cheap suit and with a bad comb-over. When he shook my hand, he let it linger until I pointedly pulled my hand from his grasp. He had a fake tan that made his skin look orange, and his teeth were impossibly white.

"Brant owns the used car lot you passed on your way into town yesterday," Ruprecht said by way of introduction.

How stereotypical; the slime ball was a used car salesman. I didn't have anything against used car salesmen, but they usually were portrayed like Brant in movies. I smiled thinly instead of speaking, and, thankfully, Brant was soon on his way.

Ruprecht leant towards me. "Not a pleasant man."

I nodded.

"Ah, here comes Craig," he said.

I followed his gaze. My heart felt as if it had stopped beating. Craig was my age, or maybe even slightly older. He was tall with an impressive build, evident even under his black suit. When he smiled, his teeth were white, but not freakishly so like Brant's. He stopped in front of me and shook my hand.

"Hi, I'm Craig," he said. "I knew your aunt."

"Thanks for coming," I said with a small smile. Craig laughed. I loved his laugh, and I was soon feeling bad for two reasons. I was making no effort to deny the fact that Craig was gorgeous, and I was already thinking about how great it would be to be romantically involved, right next to my aunt's grave. Secondly, I had just been through a bad break up. I didn't need to be worried about another man. I needed to spend time on myself.

"You're going to take over the cake store?" Craig asked.

"It sure looks that way," I said. I still hadn't even seen the place.

"Let me leave you two to it." Ruprecht placed his hand on my shoulder before walking away.

"He's a good guy," Craig said, watching the old man walk away.

"He is."

"Your aunt was one of the cornerstones of this town."

"It sounds that way. I'm sorry to say I didn't get a chance to see her much as I got older." There was no need to tell him that I didn't see her at all when I got older, and I hadn't seen her at all when I was younger, either.

"Life always gets in the way," Craig said with a smile. "This is going to make me call my family a lot more."

I nodded.

"So I bet you have a sweet tooth too, huh?" Craig asked. "I think your aunt had a cake shop just so she could eat cake all day. The woman loved what she did. She always made sure she had some mistakes, because that was what she got to snack on. It's amazing she was a skinny as she was."

"That's a tip, then," I said. "I will make mistakes so I can eat cake." I didn't tell him that my baking was always one big mistake.

Craig laughed. "I remember when I was younger, probably twelve I think, my friends and I went to the cake store. She always had those cupcakes, the chocolate cream ones. We always went outside to eat them. It's so weird how I still remember this, seeing that it's just a little sliver of my life. I remember one day when we were outside, our bikes lying all over the footpath, and we were eating the cupcakes. I turned around and there was your aunt, standing at the window, looking out at us. We had chocolate all over our faces. Your aunt was watching us, and I don't know if I had ever seen a bigger smile on someone's face. I don't think I've seen one since. She loved making people happy. There aren't many people like that, are there? All they want to do in life is make people happy."

It touched my heart to hear someone speak so fondly of my aunt. I smiled and nodded as tears came to my eyes once more. Craig stepped forward and to my shock, he hugged me tightly. Gee, these country folks were friendly.

"She was a good woman," he said. He pulled away from me and smiled softly before walking off.

As I watched him leave, I noticed a man by the nearby oak tree staring straight at me. He was tall and dark, dressed all in black. His eyes were appraising, narrowed and cold.

A chill ran up my spine.

CHAPTER 5

I looked up at the bright blue sky as I walked towards my new store after the funeral that afternoon. I thought about how ironic life could be at times. Of all of the types of shops I could have inherited, it just had to be one that sold food, and at that, food that had to be baked. As I got closer, I saw the cake store for the very first time.

I studied the front of the building from afar as I made my way down the footpath towards it. For some reason, the shop's exterior reminded me of the Victorian house that I had seen when I first arrived in Bayberry Creek. It wasn't a physical like-ness. Rather, it was a strange, yet inviting, presence.

I was almost at the door when Thyme burst

through it, her arms waving erratically in the air. "Well, there you are!"

I clutched my throat, startled. "I hope I'm not late," I said, checking the time on my mobile phone.

"No," Thyme said, "but you're pretty darn close." She chuckled, and then motioned for me to follow her inside.

"This place looks beautiful from the outside," I said.

Thyme raised her eyebrows. "This is the first time you've ever seen it? Please tell me you've at least seen your new home."

I shook my head. "Not yet, but Ruprecht's taking me there after work today."

"Well, that's great, at least. I'm sure you'll be in for a pleasant surprise."

"I've already had plenty of surprises recently," I said. "And don't get me wrong; I'm happy to own a new home and a new store, but I don't think you will understand how bad I am at cooking until you try something I attempt to make."

Thyme laughed. "You can't be that bad. Baking is easy." She turned the doorknob and pushed the door open, revealing the store to me for the first time.

When I walked in and looked around, my mouth fell open. The shelves and counters of the storefront were lined with works of art. There were rows and rows of delicious looking cakes, cupcakes, and other various creations. "Wow, this isn't what I expected at all," I confessed.

"And you're only seeing it from the customer's point of view," Thyme said. "Wait until we go through everything and you get a better understanding of what goes on behind the scenes. Then you'll really be amazed."

I wasn't quite sure what Thyme meant, but I smiled. "I just hope you know how to teach a horrible cook not to burn a cake." The last thing I wanted to do was bring down such a lovely looking store all because cooking wasn't my forte.

"Don't be so hard on yourself. There's nothing to it, seriously." Thyme spun around with a broad smile on her face. "Come this way."

"I don't think you understand just how terrible my cooking actually is," I said. No one ever did, and there were really no words to explain it. I had a mental block when it came to baking, and something always went wrong, no matter how diligent I tried to be.

"You'll be fine. I promise. Just come with me."

I followed her towards the back of the store and into a kitchen. A large countertop island stood by itself in the centre of the room, with large drawers and cabinets lining its exterior. Three ovens sat next to each other, and on the opposite wall were refrigeration units.

"So, these are the ovens," Thyme said.

I nodded. I was a bad cook, but that much I did know.

Thyme pulled open one of the oven doors to give me a look inside. "When we have a lot of orders and customers coming in and out, you'll learn to love these things. We can fit about four cakes at a time if need be."

My breath caught in my throat as the thought of trying to balance four cakes at once nearly caused me to faint. "Four? Can we just start with one at a time?" I said with horror.

Thyme smiled. "I'm going to help you until you get the hang of it, but I think you'll be fine. I understand that you're apprehensive, but everything will be okay." She walked over to a group of large, square containers. "See these things? This is where we keep the fondant."

I frowned. "What's fondant?"

Thyme laughed. "Well, think of it as an edible

icing that allows you to sculpt cakes to look however you wish. The possibilities are endless, but only if your imagination is as well. Angelica created a special recipe for her fondant. Most people use sugar and water and work with just that, but she added something that brings her cakes to life in ways other stores just can't."

Confused once again, I looked at Thyme and shrugged. A wave of nausea hit me as I came face to face with reality: I was going to have to live up to Aunt Angelica's customers' high expectations, despite the fact that I could not boil an egg without making it explode.

"You seem to be stressing yourself out over trivial things," Thyme said, oblivious to my distress. "Your aunt left this store to you for a reason, Amelia. There's something about her that you should know. This store meant the world to her. It was everything to that woman. She wouldn't have left something so precious to you if she didn't have complete faith in you." Thyme smiled widely.

Aunt Angelica left the store to me because I was her only living relative, I thought, but aloud said, "That's easier said than done," thinking about my ex-boyfriend and how my failure at baking had sent him to the hospital with food poisoning.

"Nonsense. But anyway, let's get back to business. These containers are where we store the fondant that we make for the day. It's usually one of the first things we do in the morning. We have to make enough to last throughout the entire day. Oh, and never refrigerate it. I accidentally did that once and Aunt Angelica was not happy," Thyme said with a laugh. "Anyway, always seal it tightly in Saran wrap or a Ziploc bag. Then, just toss it in these air-tight containers and it'll be good for the day."

I took mental notes of each thing that Thyme explained to me, but trying to remember minor steps and details had always been a difficult task for me. "Okay, got it. Is there anything else I should know?"

Thyme laughed. "How about actually learning to bake?"

My face went blank as I realised what was about to happen. "Now?"

"Duh. The most important part about running a cake store is making the cakes," Thyme said with a chuckle. "Let's see what we have on the itinerary today." She walked over to the countertop and pulled open one of the drawers. I peered over her shoulder and saw that it was actually a filing cabinet. "These are the orders that need to be made today," Thyme said, as she pulled out a sheet of paper and handed to me.

I looked over the order and noticed the customer's name at once. "We're making a cake for that guy?"

Thyme grinned. "Brant McCallum? Yes, he's getting married soon, so we're in charge of the wedding cake."

I wrinkled my forehead and sighed. "I've only met him at Aunt Angelica's funeral, but he seems like a bit of a creep."

"Well, he's not exactly the nicest guy in town, but he's a customer so we have to pretend we like him even if we don't. We won't have to deal with him much longer, though, so don't worry about that. Today we're just going to make a sampler so he and his fiancée can pick out which cake they want for the big day."

"Oh," I said, looking back down at the sheet of paper. The instructions were concise and the list of ingredients was carefully typed in bold print. "I already have a bad feeling about this," I said.

"No need," Thyme insisted. "Just pay attention to what I do. I'll do it all."

I nodded with relief and watched as Thyme

sprang into action. She darted around the kitchen, choosing various ingredients from the shelves and spice racks. She pulled open one of the cabinets under the countertop and selected a few baking utensils and a large mixing bowl. She plopped the items on the counter and smiled at me as she walked by. Thyme then pulled a few latex gloves from a dispenser near the sink, and tossed a pair to me. "Now you can help."

I squeezed my hands into the gloves and tried to ready myself mentally for the cooking. I stood beside Thyme and looked over the recipe one more time. "What is that ingredient?" I said, pointing at a strange word that I'd never seen before. I looked again. "Is that written in a different language?"

I received no response, so I looked over to see Thyme pouring flour into the large bowl. When she finished, she leant over towards me and looked at the word to which I was pointing. "Oh, that's just an old term for one of Aunt Angelica's special ingredients. She writes in Latin for the ones that she wants to keep private."

I wasn't sure what to make of Thyme's remark, but I just took her word for it and brushed it off. "Okay, can I help?"

"I just threw the flour in. Could you get some

eggs from the refrigerator, please?" Thyme said, pointing at the large units that I had noticed earlier.

I took out a tray of eggs and headed back to the counter. I gently set down the eggs as Thyme began narrating her every step. "So, after the flour, we have to add the vanilla extract and the eggs," she said, pouring a small amount of brown liquid over the flour and then breaking four eggs over the mixture.

After the batter was prepared, I finally began to feel more confident that I wouldn't be asked to do anything. Thyme laid out several cake pans on the countertop, and then basted each of the pans.

"Now this is the part where you'll mess up, if at all," she said to me. She then pointed to a small electronic device that sat on the wall next to the line of ovens. "Always add the exact time that Angelica put on the recipe. I'm sure you'll have to create your own recipes someday, but for now she's done all the hard work. All you have to do is follow her directions to the letter."

I nodded. I watched as Thyme poured the batter into the pans and placed them in the ovens.

After the cakes had cooled, Thyme walked me through the basic icing process. "Since these are just samples, we don't have to pull out the fondant and make them look amazing, but we still want them to look delicious and intriguing."

I nodded and watched as Thyme used an icing bag to decorate the samples.

The rest of the morning was spent with me watching Thyme bake and serve customers. We had just gone into the little back room used as the staff kitchen when the bell sounded. Thyme sighed. "Typical. A customer, right when we want to have lunch. It's probably our guy for the samples," she said, grabbing the box before leaving the kitchen.

I followed her back out to the storefront, and when I walked out, I saw Brant McCallum standing in front of the display case. "Good day, ladies," he mumbled, looking us up and down.

I wasn't quite sure what it was about the man that gave me chills, but I just didn't feel right when I was around him.

"Here are your samples," Thyme said, indicating the sample box that she placed on the counter.

Brant looked at the cakes. I could tell he didn't seem impressed. "My fiancée, Laura, seems to prefer the double chocolate, which I see one or two of in there, but I'd rather have the mocha any day of the week. I figured I'd let her choose the cake though, since it'll be the last time she'll be making any decisions at all." He laughed nastily, showing a row of his large white teeth, and then pulled out one of the samples. "See, you can always tell the difference between the mocha and the chocolate by the consistency."

I wanted nothing more than to be done with the man. I turned away, intending to leave, but I was stopped by the sound of a hacking cough. When I looked back, Brant was lying on his back on the floor. He twitched violently, and then stopped moving.

CHAPTER 6

I couldn't bear to go out into the show room, considering there was a dead body lying out there on the tiled floor. So instead, I stayed in the back, sitting on a brown stool and breathing into the paper bag that Thyme had given me. Thyme was out in the show room, past the swinging doors, waiting for the police to arrive.

By the time they did arrive, I felt marginally better. At least I didn't have to breathe into a paper bag anymore. My head was buried in my hands with my elbows on my knees when I heard the swinging doors open. I looked up and saw two cops, both in blue uniforms. A man and a woman. The man was in his forties and had bushy eyebrows as black as the hair on his head. His chest was large and barrel-like, and he looked very strong. The woman had a wide smile, but her eyes looked stern.

"Are you Amelia Spelled?" the woman asked, and I nodded. "Mind if we ask you some questions?"

I shook my head. Of course, I knew the police would need to ask me questions, and I knew there wouldn't be much point in putting it off. I would rather get it over with, and then maybe they could work on getting the dead man out of my brand new business, a business, of course, that I didn't know how to run.

The cops stopped in front of me. The man introduced himself as Sergeant Greer and the female officer as Constable Stevens.

"We talked to your employee," Greer said, hitching a thick thumb over a broad shoulder. "She's going to give us a few minutes."

It was odd to think of Thyme as my employee, and for a moment I thought they had the wrong person. I had never been someone's boss before.

"Oh," I said. It was all my muddled brain could think of at the time.

"You know the man out here?" Greer asked, flipping through a few pages of the small notebook he had produced from one of his pockets. He licked the tip of a pen and prepared to write my answer.

"I met him yesterday, at the funeral," I said.

The woman cop nodded. "Your aunt died, right?"

"Yes."

"I'm sorry to hear that," Constable Stevens said, again with the wide smile.

"Your aunt left you this place?" Greer asked, his voice scratchy and gruff, matching his eyebrows perfectly.

"Yes," I said.

"You bake cakes?"

"I guess so," I said.

The male cop lifted one of those brows, an inquisitive look. "What's that mean? 'I guess so'?"

I was irritated by the question. "I mean, I was left this business by my aunt. I have no idea how to bake cakes."

"So why not sell it?" Greer asked. "A nice little place like this! Why, you could sell it and go back to where you came from."

I shook my head. I did not want to tell them the whole sordid story of what led to me moving to town. I simply said. "It was my aunt's wish that I stay and run the business."

"That's good of you," Constable Stevens said, smiling again.

I wished she would stop smiling all the time. No one smiled that much in real life, and her smile did not look genuine. It creeped me out.

Greer went on with his questions. "You know the guy's name? The deceased man in your store out there?"

"Brant," I said. "McMurphy?"

"McCallum," Greer corrected me.

I nodded. "Right."

"He took a bite of your cake and keeled over, huh?"

"Yes, he took a bite and looked at me oddly. His eyes widened; he clutched at his throat, and he fell," I said, and suddenly I was reliving it all. For one wild moment I was sure I would need that paper bag again. I reached for it but then stopped myself. I took a deep breath, and tried to get myself back under control.

"She must really not know what she's doing," Constable Stevens said under her breath to Greer, who shot her a warning look.

"I did not bake the cake he ate!" I exclaimed, but then realised that Thyme had.

Greer towered over me. "Is there any of the

cake he ate left?"

I nodded. "A little. He was testing samples."

"What was he sampling cakes for?" Stevens asked.

"He was getting married," I said, and tears welled up in my eyes. I hadn't particularly liked Brant, but he was getting married. It was a terrible situation. I thought about his poor fiancée, and wondered if she'd heard the terrible news yet.

"Brant has some money," Greer went on. "Well, he did, at least. A lot of people would have liked to get their hands on it. Do you think anyone was out to get him?"

I was surprised the cop had asked me that. Was it a trick question? "How would I know?" I said. "I just arrived in town. I've only just met everyone."

Greer nodded and wrote something in his notebook. "Have you ever been to town before?"

"No, it's my first time," I said.

"But your aunt lived here her whole life?" Greer barked at me. "You never visited?"

"No," I said simply.

"She left you her business?"

"My father was Aunt Angelica's brother, but they didn't get along. I was surprised when I got the letter in the mail."

Neither of the police officers said anything for a moment. Both just nodded. Finally, Constable Stevens spoke. "I'm going to go bag that cake, and speak to Thyme."

"Can I go now?" I asked her. For some reason I thought everything would have taken longer.

"I need your number," Greer said.

I gave it to him.

"This place will need to stay closed for a while. A couple of days, I mean," Greer said as Constable Stevens made her way back through the swinging doors.

"Oh, okay, that's fine, of course," I said.

"There's a forensics team on the way, so you'll need to vacate the crime scene."

"Crime scene?" I heard my voice come out shrilly, and the room appeared to spin slowly. I felt like I was in a bad dream, and I couldn't wake up. "It's a crime scene?"

Greer's expression did not change. "It's routine, ma'am. You said he took a bite of cake and then fell down to the floor and died."

"But Thyme made that cake this morning. We were the only ones who touched it. So it wasn't the cake; it had to be something else."

Greer nodded, as if he had heard a million

excuses about a million different things. "You do know not to leave town?"

"Do you think I did this?" I asked, reaching for the paper bag. I felt as if I were on the edge of breaking down into hysterics.

"Routine," he said again. "Don't leave town. I'll need to escort you out so you don't contaminate the scene. Go get your things."

I waited for a few moments until I was sure that I wouldn't faint, and then I took a deep breath and climbed to my feet.

After I retrieved my handbag and coat from the back room, I slipped through the swinging doors and almost turned right back around when I saw Brant, dead, and still lying on the floor. Thyme was outside, her back pressed against the glass door of the cake store. I hurried to the door, averting my eyes from the corpse as I did so. I pulled the door slowly, so Thyme wouldn't fall if the door was gone from her suddenly.

She turned around. "Did they give you the third degree?"

I nodded. "Pretty much. And they told me not to leave town."

"Me, too."

Just then, men in white suits wheeled the body

out, right past us and into the back of the ambulance. Before they left, they fixed strips of thick yellow and black police tape across the store's door. Passers-by stopped to stare, but Thyme simply waved to them cheerfully.

I bit my lip. "Well, that certainly won't help business. People won't want to come into the store after someone died in there, and even if they did, the police said we'd need to be closed for a couple of days. Obviously they want to collect…" my voice trailed away, "evidence, I suppose."

Thyme shook her head. "Don't worry, all right? It will all be okay."

"I can't see how. I've had enough shocks lately," I said, and fought the urge to cry.

Thyme smiled. "Trust me."

"All right," I said. I couldn't see how it would be okay.

"You're seeing your house for the first time this afternoon, aren't you?" Thyme continued.

"Yes, Ruprecht will be here any minute. I'm going to follow him there." That thought cheered me up. I didn't care what the house looked like. The main thing was that Aunt Angelica had owned it outright. I never thought I'd own my own house, not in a million years.

CHAPTER 7

I couldn't believe my eyes when Ruprecht slowed his car and pulled into a driveway. It was the same house I had seen the day before, the Victorian home on one floor, with the tin roof. There was that charming little porch on the side, and the front of the house was partially obscured by pretty blue wisterias in full flower.

Ruprecht parked and got out, and I pulled up alongside his car so he would be able to get out when the time came.

"Here it is," Ruprecht said with a smile, waving an age-spotted hand towards the home. "What do you think?"

"I love it," I said, as I clasped my hands together. I was overcome with delight. "I saw it yesterday, and I loved it then. It had a pull with me." I didn't feel the need to tell Ruprecht about my GPS malfunctioning, and how it had brought me past my destination and right to this house.

As I made my way to Ruprecht, past the heavenly scent of the lilac-flowered buddleia trees, he held out a key to me. "Do the honours," he said.

I took the key and laughed, momentarily forgetting that a man had died in my cake store that day, on the first day I had ever worked in it. I slid the key into the lock that sat above the gold door handle, and turned it to the left. There was a satisfying click as a thick deadbolt slid out of place. I turned the handle and went inside.

I gasped. It was magnificent. The hallway was grand, the typical hallway of an Australian Victorian home that ran from the front to the back door in a straight line. The ceilings were twelve feet high, all pressed metal. The cornices were truly ornate. The floorboards looked like the original tallow wood boards. They were polished and covered in part by a long carpet runner in an arabesque pattern of blues and greens. The paint on the upper part of the hallway was salmon-pink: not to my taste, but hey, I was hardly going to complain. I was still pinching myself that I had a roof over my head, and a mortgage-free one at that.

Ruprecht gave me the tour. The first door on the left opened onto the living room. There was a wide bay window overlooking the front lawn, and an open brick fireplace sat at a funny angle across the far corner. At the back of the room was a door leading into a dining room. This room was smaller, but large enough for the huge table already in it. I was so lucky that the whole place was furnished.

Several bedrooms ran off the right side of the hallway. I think I counted four. Aunt Angelica's old bedroom was on the left of the hallway at the back of the house, so I thought I'd claim the bedroom at the front of the house as my own. It had a beautiful leadlight window and a small bay window over-looking the front garden. It didn't have an en-suite bathroom, although the main bathroom was right next to it.

The main bathroom had a delightful claw-foot bath and white tiles. It had clearly been renovated in recent times. The ceiling was again pressed metal, complete with a magnificent ceiling rose.

"And this is the library," Ruprecht said, opening a door off the hallway. He gasped. "My mistake; I must be thinking of a different house." He shot me a funny look.

"There's a library?" I asked.

Again the funny look. "Um, err, I don't remember," Ruprecht said, hurrying on down the long hall.

I was pretty sure he was lying, but I had no idea why. It made no sense. Was he suffering from memory loss and not wanting to admit it?

The kitchen was the second to last room on the left. It was somewhat dated, but again, I was the last one to complain. At least it didn't have smoke damage all over the ceiling. Behind the kitchen was a cute little room. Every room in the house had a fireplace, so, when Ruprecht showed me out the back, I was surprised to see a tiny wood box under the back veranda and no wood shed.

"Where did Aunt Angelica keep her firewood?" I asked Ruprecht.

He nodded to the wood box. "There."

I scratched my head. "That's only big enough for two or three days. Didn't she get a whole load delivered at once? I can't see anywhere to put it."

Again, the same funny look crossed Ruprecht's face. "I'll explain it all before winter. There's plenty of time to think of that. You have so much on your mind now." He wrung his hands in a nervous gesture. "Well, I can leave you to it," he said, one eyebrow twitching. "I'm sure you'd like to get a few things settled. I'll check in on you in a day or two."

I smiled and nodded. "Thank you," I said. "For everything."

Ruprecht simply waved his hand through the air. "Don't mention it!"

I walked him to the front and watched him drive off before I started unpacking my car.

It didn't have much, only my clothes, make up, laptop, and few boxes of various belongings. Still, the car was bursting at the seams. I figured you never really know just how much stuff you have until you move.

By the time I had unpacked my belongings, such as they were, it was all beginning to sink in. I had moved from a big city on the coast to a small, inland country town in the middle of nowhere. I had gained a mortgage-free house and a business— even though that business did involve baking—and I was sure I had found new friends. I had even seen a hot guy. Who knew small country towns had them? It all more than made up for losing Brad, losing my job, and getting evicted. Still, a man had died today, and I was still shaken.

When I'm upset, I usually have a glass of wine, a lot of ice cream and/or chocolate, or a long, hot bubble bath. I had no wine or ice cream, and I'd had no time to do any shopping. I'd packed a large supply of jelly beans and my coffee machine, along with plenty of coffee. I figured a bath would be just the thing. I was keen to try out the old tub with the claw feet in the bathroom.

I don't know how long I stayed in the bath, but by the time I got out and pulled on my pyjamas, the sky outside was dark. I went into the living room and turned on the TV, and was delighted to see that Aunt Angelica had Netflix. Before I could decide what to watch, there was a knock on the door.

I went to it slowly, and opened the door a crack.

"Camino," I said.

"Yes, you got it," the elderly woman said. I had met her at my aunt's funeral, and the strange but beautiful little ceremony beforehand. Tonight Camino was dressed in a similar fashion, though there was a splash of colour in all the white by way of a purple blouse. She held a cardboard box before her, open, with two cats sitting inside.

"Would you like to come in?" I asked, wondering if everyone in these parts took their cats with them when visiting.

"Certainly, dear," Camino said. "Thank you."

"I'm afraid I don't have much," I said. "I could

find some coffee, I'm sure. There are jelly beans, too."

"No, thank you," Camino said, as she set the box on the floor and then sat on the couch.

I sat opposite her in a huge, old armchair upholstered wildly in primary colours.

"You don't already have a pet, do you?" Camino asked. "A dog?"

I shook my head. "No, I couldn't have them in my old apartment. Any pet. They were very strict about it."

Camino nodded hard, and snorted. "I've been taking care of these cats since your aunt crossed over. They were your aunt's, and I'm afraid they miss her something awful."

"I'm sure it must be hard," I said, feeling sorry for the poor creatures.

"Well, to cut to the chase, dear, I need you to have them. I take in a lot of animals. I live next door. You passed the house when you drove up. I like to take care of animals, but you can only have so many in your home before you have to start wondering if you're living in a zoo. They were your aunt's, and now they are yours."

I looked at the box. Both cats were large adults.

One was fat, orange and white, and the other, slender and all black.

"I've never really had a pet," I said, "although I've always wanted pets." I was delighted.

"Cats are easy to care for," Camino said.

"What are their names?"

Camino pointed to the orange cat. "Willow," she said. She pointed to the black cat. "Hawthorn."

"My aunt must have liked her trees, huh?"

"I guess so," Camino said.

"I hope the cats like me and don't run away or anything."

Camino shook her head. "They're your familiars now, dear."

"I'm not familiar with them at all, though, is what I'm saying," I argued. I wanted to be a responsible pet owner, after all. "I'm not familiar with them, or cats in general."

"No, honey." Camino laughed heartily. "They were your aunt's familiars, and now they're yours."

I shook my head. Perhaps old age had made her slightly potty. "I'm sure she was familiar with them, but I'm not. I'm sorry."

Camino stood up. She looked at me and tilted her head slightly. "You don't know anything about this, do you?"

"That's what I'm trying to tell you. I don't know anything about raising cats." I said, throwing up my hands.

This just seemed to amuse Camino more, and she began to laugh again. She went for the door. "Just feed them, and keep water in their bowl, and they'll do most everything else," she said before she left.

I shut the door behind her and then went back to the couch. I looked down into the box and the cats looked up at me. Willow meowed, and Hawthorn jumped into my lap.

I needn't have worried; the cats seemed delighted to see me. They purred all over me. "Want some dinner? Has Camino already fed you?"

The big ginger cat meowed. "Okay, come with me," I said. I found some cans of cat food in the tiny kitchen. I opened them and set them on the white linoleum tiles. I filled two bowls with water, and then I went to my bedroom.

The cats followed me in. One, the big one, of course, sat on my stomach, and the other tried to lick my face. I tried to roll on my side, but that angered the one sitting on my legs, and he swiped at me. And so I lay perfectly still in the darkness, staring up at the ceiling. I thought of my mother. I didn't know why I did, and I wondered if it was something to do with wanting to think of my aunt but not knowing anything about her.

So instead I thought of my mother. I thought of one time when I was nine, and my father had let me watch a scary movie. My mother had told him not to do it, but my father was stubborn and laughed it off. He said I was old enough not to be scared by a silly movie.

Yet it *had* frightened me, and when I was put to bed that night, I called out within a minute of my light being turned off and my door shut. The shadows on the walls all at once had seemed menacing. I felt like I was being watched.

My mother came in, and I could see by her face that she was mad at my father, not at me.

"What's wrong?" my mother asked me.

"The movie scared me."

Her tone softened. "I knew it would."

"Do you get scared?"

My mother didn't answer for a long time. Finally, she looked at me and nodded. "Sometimes I do."

"When?"

"I can tell you about one of the times I was the

most scared. I was about as old as you are now, maybe a little younger."

"Okay, tell me," I had begged.

"I was walking home from violin practice," my mother began. "Practice was at Mrs Seymour's house. She lived a few blocks away. I didn't want to learn to play the violin, but my mother made me take the lessons."

"Why?" I asked.

"Sometimes we parents think we know better than our children."

"Don't you?"

"Usually," my mother said with a laugh. "Now hush and listen. I always cut through yards to get to her house, and back to mine, but one day, as I opened a gate and went into a yard I had cut through a hundred times, I heard a loud barking. Whoever had lived in the house had a new dog. I saw him, coming at me. He was big with sharp, white teeth. I turned to go for the gate, but somehow I couldn't open it. My hands weren't working. I felt the dog close behind me. I turned, and his face was right near mine. I was shaking. He opened his mouth, and then he licked me."

I had giggled.

"That's when I knew not everything scary was

worth worrying about," my mother continued. "The movie was scary, but it's not real, so it's not worth worrying about, right?"

When my mother left the room, I still felt as if something was watching me. I didn't want to call her back, so I pulled the blankets over my head.

Right now, I had the same feeling. I dislodged myself from the cats, and crossed to the curtains. I pulled one aside, and under the streetlight, there was a figure, the tall, dark figure of a man. A chill ran right through me, and I jumped back from the curtain. When I looked again, he was gone.

CHAPTER 8

From time to time as the morning went on, I sat by the bay window looking out over the front garden. I was awaiting news from the police station to tell me when I would be able to reopen the cake store. I was concerned that the police would find something deadly in the cakes that had killed Brant McCallum, but that was unlikely, since I hadn't baked them.

I had walked the three blocks to the local store to buy necessities such as microwave dinners, chocolate, and ice cream, and then spent the morning exploring the garden. I was thrilled to have a garden of my own.

In one of my moments sitting by the bay window, the sound of my new cats tearing through the house shattered my quiet contemplation. I leaped to my feet and headed in the direction of the screeching cats. They were not in the hallway, and for a moment all was quiet. Then the sound started again, pulling my attention to a door on the left of the hallway.

I opened the door expecting to see another bedroom, but it was a library. I did a double take. How had I overlooked this room? Sure, the house was rambling, but I thought I had seen all the rooms. I was sure this was the one that had made Ruprecht pause. Yet, he had said that the room wasn't a library. I thought we had then gone into the room, and found it was another bedroom, but then again, I must have been confused. Perhaps Ruprecht had shut the door and we'd gone on to the next bedroom.

If that were the case, why would Ruprecht try to hide the library from me when I would find it anyway? I had no idea. Even trying to figure it out was giving me a headache.

I rubbed my forehead and walked into the room. There were shelves upon shelves of books. I walked over to a shelf and picked up the first book I saw. It was a heavy book, brown leather with the words, *Aristotle, Metaphysics*, embossed in gold writing. I quickly put it back. The next book was entitled, *Papyri Graecae Magicae: the Greek Magical Papyri in Translation*. I put it back, too. Aunt Angelica sure wasn't into simple romances.

Before I could look at any more books, the cats ran past me. The orange and white cat, Willow, sniffed and clawed at one of the bookcases. He then stood on his hind legs, almost as if he were trying to reach for a particular book. I walked towards him quietly, hoping not to startle him. Just then, I noticed the black cat, Hawthorn, walking along the shelf just above Willow.

I wasn't sure what to make of the crazy cats, so I shrugged it off and turned to go back to the living room. I had just reached the door when there was a loud thud. I swung around to see the two cats sitting on the floor next to a book. For a moment, I felt like the cats were smiling up at me.

"Well, you two are already proving to be mischievous!" I said, as I crouched down to pick up the book. I could barely make out the title, so I took it over to the window. In the light, I could just make out the words, *Book of Shadows*.

"How strange," I said aloud. What looked like a pentagram could be seen etched into the soft material of the book. I flipped open the pages and was at once surprised to see handwriting. I continued skimming through its contents, and all I found were scribbles and doodles.

Then, I realised exactly what I was looking at: a recipe book. Several herbs and other recognizable ingredients, such as sugar and coffee, were scattered throughout. I quickly slammed the book closed and sighed. I glanced down at the cats, who were both sitting at my feet, watching me intently. "Oh, you two really are going to be a handful, aren't you? You can sniff about the house all you like, but don't drag any more recipe books off the shelves!" I wagged my finger at each of the felines, and then realised I was already turning into a crazy cat lady.

I walked back towards the bookcase. As I extended my arm to put it back, I caught another glimpse of the pentagram. I didn't really know much about symbols and old secret societies and such, but the shape did remind me of something specific: a TV show I used to watch called *Ghost Chasers*. I carefully studied the pentagram, feeling the etching with my fingers as I recalled some details of the show. I remembered how they spoke of the pentagram. They said it was an ancient symbol of protection and power, although I never really understood what that had meant.

Just then, there was a loud thud on the other

side of the room. I looked to see if the cats were at it again, but they still remained by my feet. The sound pulled my memory back to the show's biggest attention-grabber: how the ghost hunters would call out and ask for a reply when they suspected an entity was present.

The eerie atmosphere of the old Victorian home was enough to scare even the biggest of sceptics. I laughed at the thought of ghosts or other apparitions haunting my new house. In a half-joking way, I repeated the show's famous line, "If you can hear me and wish to make contact, please knock once."

Suddenly, there was a loud knock at the front of the house. I clutched my stomach as the hairs on the back of my neck stood tall. My skin quickly filled with goose bumps. I went cold all over.

I quickly made for the front of the house. I reached for the door with trembling hands, and then stood there, hesitating.

I waited by the door, wondering if the sound would come again. It did, but this time, it sounded like an actual knock on my front door. I bit my lip and grasped the knob firmly, turning it slowly as I pulled the door open.

"Good morning, ma'am," Sergeant Greer said.

He was accompanied by Constable Stevens, the female cop. "May we come in?" he asked.

"Yes, of course," I replied, motioning for them to enter. I was relieved that they weren't ghostly entities. They walked in, one after the other, and then followed me towards the sofa and chairs.

"Would you like to sit down?" I asked. I wasn't used to speaking to police, so didn't know the protocol. I had watched reruns of *Midsomer Murders* many times, but that was England, not Australia.

"No, thank you," Constable Stevens replied.

"We're here to let you know what our investigation has turned up," Sergeant Greer said.

"Oh," I replied, and waited for him to continue.

Sergeant Greer chewed his lip. "We weren't able to find anything in your cakes." He sounded disappointed.

"Not a single trace of poison, mould, unsanitary food, or anything else," the female officer added, grinning broadly.

"Right. Which is why we're going to close the investigation and allow you to reopen the store," Greer said.

I was pleased to hear such positive news, but I wondered what had actually happened to Brant

McCallum. "Uh, then how did he die, if you don't mind me asking?"

The male officer leant forward and spoke in a stern tone. "The official report has his cause of death listed as ischemic heart disease, and the manner of death is natural causes. That is why we have no other choice but to allow you to reinstate your business."

"Heart disease?" I said, confused.

Greer shrugged. "It's basically the category that most common heart failures are listed under. The coroner wasn't able to pinpoint exactly what caused his heart to fail that day. She told us she did the exam twice to confirm his findings, because according to McCallum's charts, the man didn't have a history of any heart defects or disease."

"Oh," I said, turning away. As I did, I caught a quick glance of Willow and Hawthorn as they sat in a far corner of the room. I wondered if they had been sitting there the entire time I had been speaking with the police. It was strange how they were just sitting there, focused on the conversation. I turned back to the two police officers and frowned. "Obviously, I'm happy that the shop isn't to blame in any way, but it's still very upsetting that a man died right in front of my own eyes. Poor

Thyme, too." I felt tears coming on, so I sniffled into a tissue. "I'm sorry. I think I'm just still in a state of shock or disbelief or whatever."

"That's understandable," the female cop said, still smiling widely. "Death is a difficult thing for everyone. If you need any help at all, just call this number." She handed me a small, white business card. "This is a doctor who speaks to victims and their families, families of offenders, and anyone else who's been through a traumatic experience such as this."

"Oh, I think I'll be okay, thanks," I said. "I was just hoping to have a sense of closure in the matter. I was worried that it was my fault somehow, and it's great to hear otherwise, but it just doesn't make much sense. He was perfectly fine until he bit into that cake. How could it have nothing to do what happened to him?"

Sergeant Greer shook his head. "It seems like it was just a freak coincidence, to be honest. We don't have the toxicology screens back on the victim yet, but every one of those sample cakes was tested, not just the one he took a bite out of. Not one of them contained any traces of chemicals or drugs, or anything else of the sort. His heart just gave out."

I studied the officer's eyes as he spoke. I was

sure that he believed everything he was saying, but I struggled to do the same. I glanced over at Constable Stevens, who was still wearing her usual over-the-top smile. "I suppose things like that happen every day in the world," I admitted, "but I'm just not used to them happening around me."

"It was probably just a one in a million kind of thing," the woman replied. "Don't let it scare you."

I raised an eyebrow at the cop's words. I wasn't sure why the woman would have said such a thing, but it didn't sit well with me for some reason. What was there to be scared about in such a nice town?

"Thank you for your time," Sergeant Greer said, and the two officers turned to leave.

Once I closed the door behind them, I went back into the living room. Willow and Hawthorn were peering out the bay window, staring at the cops as they left.

CHAPTER 9

*B*rad had always told me that I was going to end up killing someone with my cooking. I was relieved that I hadn't proven the jerk right yet.

Yet was the operative word. Why? Why a cake shop? My food was not fit for human consumption. It was so not cake-shop quality. You don't serve cardboard flavoured bricks and iced charcoal to customers. No one would think my food was edible, much less tasty.

Regardless, it was a relief that the cake samples didn't kill the man. It would have killed me if the cakes had somehow been toxic, despite my not even touching them. I probably would never have been able to step into a kitchen again.

I took a deep breath and looked around the

house. It was still so surreal. Everything had happened so fast. One minute I had lost everything, and the next I was in a new town starting a new life, a life of baking cakes for people. Heaven help this poor town. Thank goodness for Thyme.

I almost jumped out of my skin when the home phone rang right beside me. I tensed up. Who would be calling? I hadn't given anyone here the number yet. Was it someone calling for Aunt Angelica?

"Hey," a familiar voice chimed in cheerfully as I picked up. "How are you doing?"

"Oh, Thyme, hi!" I stammered as I tried to think up what to say. Goodness, in all the chaos, I had forgotten to call Thyme and update her. She was right there when the man died, so she had to have been wondering what happened. "I'm so sorry. I meant to call you sooner."

"Don't worry about it." I could almost see Thyme wave off my apology with a graceful sweep of her hand. "I'm sure you're busy celebrating the sample cakes being cleared and all."

"Huh?" I stopped in my tracks. I myself had only just found that out. "How did you know?"

"A little bird told me." Thyme's voice had a playful tone to it. "I told you there was nothing to worry about. It was just an unhappy coincidence that he came to the shop before he died. It could have been anywhere."

"I guess." I was glad that the shop had no part in the man's death. Yet it felt wrong to celebrate that Brant McCallum had died of natural causes. It was even weirder to hear Thyme being so accepting of the whole thing. Or maybe I was the one being strange. After all, if it hadn't been natural or some sort of accident—I shook off the thought.

"Glad to hear it. So when are they going to let you reopen the shop?"

I winced. "They cleared it this morning." I needed to figure out what to do about that shop. Sure, it hadn't killed anybody, but it didn't mean I could make it succeed. It had taken two staff members, Aunt Angelica and Thyme, to run it before, and now there was only Thyme and me, and I was a serious liability. "Sorry I didn't tell you. It's no longer a crime scene, anyway."

"Great. See you there in an hour," Thyme said with the same cheerful energy. "You need to start learning to bake."

"What?" I gripped the back of a chair tightly.

"Yeah. You have to learn eventually. You have some baking to do."

"Oh no, no, Thyme. No!" I waved a finger at the air in front of me for emphasis.

"Yes, yes, yes." Despite the firmness of Thyme's voice, I could swear I heard hints of laughter in it. "There's no point in putting it off. You've inherited a cake store, so you'll have to learn to bake. No time like the present, right?"

After about five or so minutes of debate, I realised that my new friend had a stubborn streak, at least when it came to this. She was going to get me in that shop if she had to show up on my doorstep to do it.

So an hour later, I was there with my cheerful and triumphant friend, at my very own little shop of horrors, complete with tools for my mad experiments on how many ways I could ruin flour and sugar.

If Thyme noticed my misery, she didn't give any indication. "Don't worry. Baking is easy. You just have to follow the recipe."

Easy for her to say! Thyme had never made an Easy Bake Oven cry for mercy. Yet I had to admit that she did have a point. If I didn't get in there now, I was going to keep finding excuses not to do so. If I were to be honest with myself, it was nice to have someone care enough to want to help me, even if it was with something like baking.

Maybe it wouldn't be so bad.

"HOW DID YOU DO THAT?" Thyme asked me in a puzzled tone as we sat side by side on the bench, waiting for the fire department to arrive. The last remnants of smoke lazily wafted out the kitchen window.

I groaned and buried my face in both hands. I should have known that I wasn't magically going to learn to bake that easily, even with close supervision. "Sorry."

Thyme waved away the apology and seemed more amused than anything. "It's not like it was a big disaster or anything. We put the flames out easily. I wouldn't even have called anyone in if you didn't need the report. Insurance won't replace the oven without it."

I was horrified. "The oven might need to be replaced?"

Thyme shrugged. "No idea, but it *is* an old oven. Angelica had it for years. You might do better with one that you feel a good vibe with, and it would be better if the insurance bought it for you, right?" Thyme gave a playful wink and then fanned away a cloud of smoke that drifted our way.

I suspected that she was just trying to cheer me up. Still, it was nice to have someone supportive in my corner during my latest cooking incident. "It's hopeless." I sighed and glanced over my shoulder at the store. Why couldn't my aunt have left me a bookstore? A shoe store? Anything but a cake store?

"Not at all." Thyme followed my gaze and gave a half smile. "Good thing Aunt Angelica kept three ovens for busy times. We'll use a less temperamental one after they have a look at the kitchen."

"Do we have to?" I fixed an exaggerated tragic expression on my face, trying to lighten things despite my worries. I had to smile as Thyme let out a laugh.

"You'll get it. I have feelings about these things. And you, Amelia Spelled, are going to make the most amazing cakes ever."

When Thyme said things in that confident tone of hers, it was hard not to believe it. But of course, I had months of proof to the contrary. "I'm afraid that's a bet you're going to lose."

"Oh no, I'm not allowed to bet. It's frowned upon in this establishment." Thyme spoke in a mock dignified tone as she pretended to look over an imaginary pair of glasses.

"What establishment?" I asked her. Sounds like this town was pretty old fashioned in the gambling department.

Thyme gave me a grin and leant over to rest her chin on her hands. "I was only joking, but we're getting off topic. You *are* going to be a great cook. I would bet on it."

"Nice of you to say."

"Nope." Thyme shook her head. "Not just saying. *Knowing*. After all, you have people to help you learn now. It's a huge difference from reading stuff on the web."

"Teach me, Master Yoda," I said, giving a playful bow of homage. I wished I had Thyme's confidence, but at the moment I'd settle for her good company.

"Ha, I'm just here to help you get your start," Thyme said. "You'll do great. Trust me on this."

"Any hints how?" I couldn't help but sigh at the thought of it.

"First off, every ingredient has its place in the recipe. Eggs bind. Yeast makes it fluff. Sugar sweetens. The list goes on. Same for the tools. Everything is there for its own reason. Trust the recipe and you won't go wrong."

I suppressed a sigh. "If only it were that easy." If it were as easy as following instructions, I would have nailed it long ago.

"It is. Well it isn't. But it is." Thyme bit her bottom lip thoughtfully. "It's not so much mimicking the words, as feeling it."

Okay, that was about as clear as mud.

Thyme must have realised it by the look on her face. "Okay, um, it isn't just mixing eggs and flour for example." Thyme waved her hands helplessly as she tried to find the words. "It's feeling the mix get smooth while you stir it. It's sensing that exact moment it changes from powder and goo into batter. Things they just can't teach someone on a recipe card."

It was all sounding horribly complicated to me. "But how does anyone ever learn such a thing?"

"Trial and error," Thyme said matter of factly. "Lots of trial and error. And love. Love is the secret ingredient."

"Love?" I raised my eyebrows. We had gone from a serious lesson to some sickening sweet cliché from those cooking shows that Brad had made me watch.

Thyme smiled. "Your aunt always said it was her secret weapon. When you make something with love, you have a completely different energy. You're more alert. You see small details. Time passes differently. It's totally different from making something out of obligation."

I thought that over. Had I tried to cook for Brad because I loved him at the time? Or because I felt like it was expected of me? At the time I had thought it was one and the same. I didn't even really know if this whole 'love' thing made sense to me now.

"But how do you love cooking for a complete stranger?" I asked, looking back over at the cake shop. Even if I bought into the whole 'love makes the recipe perfect' thing, how did that fit with dealing with customers?

I thought back on my work at the Complaints Department, where I was cursed at and lectured by customers over the company's flaws as if I were the one directly responsible. Customers yelled at me if their demands were not met immediately. I thought of the apartment where the landlord kicked me out as soon as I set the place on fire, and how Brad abandoned me because I gave him food poisoning.

"To tell the truth, I'm not sure. That was your

aunt's talent." Thyme gave me an apologetic half-shrug. "She baked with her emotions, and it showed in her cakes. That's really all I know. As to how she channelled that love into her work—well, you'll have to find your own way there."

I threw up my hands. "Great!"

"You'll be fine. You'll just need to—oh, finally. It's a good thing this wasn't a serious fire. You'd be less a shop." Thyme nodded to the fire truck as it finally swung into the street.

I smiled and stood up beside her. While I did not relish letting the fire department see my burned cake, I was glad for a distraction from the conversation.

"You guys take the scenic route?" Thyme asked pleasantly.

One of the men hopped out of the truck and made his way over, while the others went straight for the kitchen. "Sorry, ladies. We had to take the long way due to the high school parade taking up the main street."

"Oh, yeah." Thyme bonked herself on the forehead. "I saw it in the news feed. I completely forgot about it. Guess this wasn't the best day for a cooking lesson. Sorry, guys."

I smiled and shook my head.

"I haven't ever been called out here before," the man commented as he removed his hat to get a better look at the window. "Is everyone all right?"

I felt my heart leap in my chest as his deep brown eyes met mine. This was the hot guy I had met at the funeral.

"Umm, yes. Yes. I just set a cake on fire, but it's all under control now," I said. Oh no, I had just admitted that I burned a cake. How incompetent did that sound? Why did I open my mouth?

Craig smiled in amusement. "Well, it can't be any worse than when Angelica started this store decades ago. My grandfather told me that when she heard you use a torch to do meringue she borrowed one from a welding shop."

I didn't know what the difference in torches was, but based on his grin and Thyme's wide-eyed alarmed giggle, I assumed it ran along the lines of 'overkill.'

"My aunt burned cakes?" I asked.

"And half the wall," he said. "A table too, if my grandfather was correct. In the end, she made the best cakes. It's good to see her legacy is going to live on."

"See? Trial and error. *Lots* of error." Thyme laughed and elbowed me.

I laughed, too. I was glad to see that Craig was okay with me setting a cake on fire.

"Oh, welcome to Bayberry Creek. I can't remember if I said that when we first met." Craig didn't take his eyes off mine. What amazing eyes. "I'm glad to see this place is okay," he continued. "I'll check it out, just to be on the safe side."

"Thanks." I smiled at him. "Thyme says we need the report for insurance."

Thyme raised her eyebrows at me and then put her hands behind her back with a mischievous smile. "Well, I'm going to go check on progress with the kitchen. Amelia, how about you tell him what happened?" Thyme leant in to whisper to me, "And find out his favourite flavour."

CHAPTER 10

I had invited Thyme, Ruprecht, his granddaughter, Mint, and my next-door neighbour, Camino, over for dinner. It wasn't my idea; it was Thyme's. She said it was the only way I could get my confidence. She suggested I make something simple. Duh! I knew that much.

I decided to make baked vegetables. I stood in the kitchen, my eyes closed, my hands on the counter. "You can do this," I chanted over and over.

I opened my eyes, and got to work. For the first ten minutes or so everything was going great. Of course, the first ten minutes were the easiest, chopping up the vegetables. From there it got a little harder, and as I had dreaded, I began to feel like I wasn't doing it right. I had partly boiled the potatoes first, as the article on the net had said that they take longer to cook than other vegetables. Had I boiled them for too long? Were they supposed to break apart?

I was beginning to sweat, though it wasn't only due to the oven being cranked to four fifty. I was starting to feel the panic. I wanted to do well. I owned a cake store, after all.

Now my new friends were going to come over, and I was surely going to mess it all up. I forced myself to think logically. What was the worst that could happen? That thought calmed me down somewhat. So what if I messed up dinner? Thyme wouldn't be mad, and Ruprecht wouldn't ridicule me with cruel words, not like my ex had. If dinner was ruined, they would all laugh.

I had just put the chopped up pumpkin into the oven when the doorbell rang. I wiped my hands on a towel hanging on the handle of the oven and went to answer it. Ruprecht and Mint stood before me, a smile on their faces. "House-warming gift," Ruprecht said, holding out a box of rather nice antique silverware. "I had it at the shop, and I thought it would look lovely here with you."

"Wow, thanks so much," I said, taking the box.

"I didn't bring anything, only this bottle of chardonnay," a cheerful voice said from behind

Ruprecht. Thyme was making her way up the front walk. She had a huge bag in one hand and bottle of wine in the other.

"Thanks," I said with a laugh. "Come on in. Camino should be here soon. Let me check on the veggies, and I'll be right back."

I hurried into the kitchen and anxiously peered into the oven. To my relief, nothing was burned yet. It appeared to be roasting to plan.

I returned to the living room with a tray of wine glasses. I was almost at the living room door when I heard Camino's voice. Oh, good, she had arrived. The next words I heard made me stop in my tracks.

"Yes, I saw him, parked down the street in his car," Camino said.

"Are you sure it was him?" Ruprecht asked.

"Positive. What would he want with Amelia?"

From behind me, Willow meowed loudly. I was afraid he would give away my position, and I felt bad for eavesdropping, so I walked into the room.

Everyone stopped talking abruptly and stared at me. You could cut the tension with a knife. "What were you all talking about?" I asked.

"Nothing," Thyme and Mint said in unison, and then they exchanged glances. I saw a red flush travel up Thyme's face.

"Great, wine glasses," Camino said, in what seemed to me to be an obvious attempt to divert me. "Do you have red? I'm partial to Merlot."

"Sure," I said, and took everyone's orders.

"So you found Angelica's wine supply?" Camino asked me, her eyes narrowing as if the answer was of importance to her.

"Yes," I said.

"You didn't have any trouble finding it? You've found your way around the house okay?" she asked, and Ruprecht shot her what to me looked like a warning look. This was getting stranger and stranger.

"You look somewhat stressed," Ruprecht said, as he accepted his glass from me. "I hope you aren't going to too much trouble for us."

"No, no trouble at all," I assured him. "Just way out of my league."

"You? Out of your league in the kitchen?" Thyme teased me. "I never would have guessed."

"Very funny," I said. "When the rest of us are eating a delicious meal, and you've been sent to a timeout with no dinner, don't be mad at me."

"I'm actually really looking forward to it," Thyme said. "I'm proud of you for taking on some-thing head on. I hope it goes well."

"So far, so good," I said hopefully.

Half an hour later, I was in the kitchen staring at some blackened vegetables burned to a crisp, and potatoes which had somehow turned to mush in the exact same oven. I felt like I wanted to cry. How had this happened?

I turned and went to the dining room, where Ruprecht, Thyme, Mint, and Camino sat at the table.

"I guess we can order a pizza," I said, trying to smile, but feeling horrible.

Thyme stood up. "It's okay. Besides, I did bring something."

Thyme opened her large bag that was sitting on the table and pulled out another bag, this one white. "Veggie burgers," she said, and then she laughed. "Just in case."

I couldn't help but laugh. I had messed up dinner, just the way I had thought I would, but no one was mad. It was funny, silly, and Thyme had thought ahead to save the day, but in a way that didn't make me feel an inch tall. The five of us laughed as I sat down at the table.

"No faith in me, huh?" I joked.

"I have a lot of faith in you," Thyme said. "I just knew your oven would be on the fritz."

"Yeah, that's what it was," I said for a joke. "Sure, the oven was messed up."

"You can't trust old things," Ruprecht said. "Like me. I'm liable to break down at any moment too."

We all laughed. And so we spent the evening eating burgers from a local fast food joint, and laughing and telling stories. Ruprecht had a lot of life to share, and the rest of us listened to him speak with rapt attention.

And then the talk turned to my aunt. They had all known her well. I hadn't known my aunt at all, and listening to stories about her made me smile. By the time they had finished speaking about her, my cheeks hurt from smiling. "She sounds amazing," I said.

"She was," Thyme said, and the old man next to her nodded.

"It seems to run in the family," Ruprecht added. "We're so glad you're here, dear."

"Me, too," I said. "Would anyone like coffee?"

"I'll take a cup," Ruprecht said.

"Me too," Thyme said. "You need any help?"

I burst out laughing. "Trust me. Running the coffee maker is one thing I can do in the kitchen."

Ten minutes later, I set steaming mugs in front

of everyone. "Let's sit out front," I suggested, and we all went outside. There were a few white wicker chairs out there, and we pulled them from their spot against the wall and set them up.

The night was warm with a clear sky and an almost full moon. A soft breeze blew and the nearby trees rustled pleasantly.

"I don't even miss home," I said.

Thyme smiled at me. "This is home for you now."

I nodded. "It's just weird, to spend so much time in one place, and then to leave it and realise it was never the right place for you," I said. "And then you find somewhere and you just feel like, well, I don't know, like how I feel about this place."

Ruprecht nodded in agreement. "We all feel like we belong here. Some of us are weirder than the others," he added, making a show of pointing to Thyme, which made us laugh. "But we all belong. In a way, I think this town attracts people like us, people who don't fit in other places, even if they don't know it. People who are special."

"I don't think I'm special at all," I said with a shrug. "Weird, perhaps."

"Of course you are," Ruprecht said with a twinkle in his eye. "Special, not weird, I mean."

After everyone finished their coffee, they all said their goodbyes, and I was left alone once more. I thought about what Ruprecht had said. It was such a small, throwaway line, but the way he had said it made me feel something. I didn't know what.

I could feel something coming, something big, and it would change me. I had never felt like that before, but now I felt something. I did feel special, for the first time. I hadn't felt special before, but now, in the new town and the new house, I did.

I went to bed after I cleaned up the burger wrappers left in the dining room. I lay in bed and stared at the ceiling as I drifted off to sleep, finally closing my eyes. I thought about what Ruprecht had said, until my dreams overtook me. I dreamed of doing things, things I had never done before, things I hadn't been able to do. In one dream, I told off my ex-boyfriend, loudly, with anger. In another, I cooked a beautiful meal. And in the next dream, I was alone in a room. An angry shadow loomed over me and wanted to hurt me, but I wouldn't let it. I held up a hand and light burst forth from my fingertips, and there were no more shadows. The dreams went on, and I slept well.

CHAPTER 11

*J*opened my eyes, and it took me a moment to place where I was. Actually, I couldn't quite place where I was. I was lying on a couch instead of my bed. There were two windows along one wall. The flowing white curtains hung loosely and blocked a good amount of the sunshine that was trying to squeeze through the window, leaving nothing but long rectangles of yellow which fell across the floor and the far wall.

I was in my new home. I knew this, but I wasn't in my bedroom. In fact, as I sat up on the dusty couch and looked around, I was pretty sure I had never seen the room in which I had awoken at all.

That didn't make sense. There were no real hidden rooms in houses, were there? That was just in movies, and cartoons where an animated dog solved mysteries with his human friends.

Apart from the couch, the room was mostly empty, except for a white wicker stand near the door. On the stand was a large bowl, something decorative, ceramic and white with blue lines. I moved from the couch and went to the bowl, expecting to find something in it, but I was disappointed. It was empty.

I reached for the rounded handle of the door next to the wicker stand, and for one wild moment I was worried that it would be locked. I would be stuck in this strange room, a room in my home that I was pretty sure hadn't been there when I had gone to sleep. But no, the door handle turned easily, and I pulled open the door to reveal the familiar hallway.

My heart was pounding and my forehead was sweaty. I stepped into the hall. Yes, it was indeed my hall. What a relief! My bedroom was down at the end of the hall, the bathroom with the old fashioned bathtub with clawed feet to the left of that. I turned and looked into the room in which I had awoken. It was still there. I had thought that maybe I would turn and see nothing but the wall, with the white and yellow wallpaper with the roses that ran along the top border.

But no, there it was, the couch along the far wall, the windows, the sunlight, the bowl on the wicker stand. I reached forward and pulled the door shut with a slam.

I didn't know what to think; I only knew that I was frightened. I hurried down the hallway into my bedroom. To my utter relief, this room was normal. The bed, my clothes, my mobile phone on the nightstand next to where I had laid my head, all looked normal.

I went back to the room in which I had woken up, and it was still there. I had never seen this room before. How had I missed it? I hurried down the hallway and flung open the library door. It was a bedroom. I ran up and down the hallway, flinging open all the doors, but there was no library to be found. I sunk to the floor, a wave of nausea overcoming me. I sat there for a few moments, my head in my hands. What was going on? Was I still dreaming? I pinched myself. "Ouch!" I said aloud, and Willow and Hawthorn walked over to inspect me.

One thing was for certain, I was too shaken to go to work. I went to my phone and called Thyme.

"Would you mind going in today without me? Just for a bit? Something's come up," I said.

"Are you okay?" Thyme's voice was filled with concern. "Did something happen?"

"No, I'm fine," I said, trying to convince Thyme as much as I was trying to convince myself.

Thyme hesitated for a moment. "All right. Well, I'll head on in. Call me later, okay?"

"Sure," I said. "Thanks." I sighed deeply and sat on the edge of my bed. From where I sat, I could see into the hall and see the door that led to the mysterious new room.

I wasn't going crazy, was I? I knew I hadn't simply missed that room in the days since I had moved in. It was so close to my own bedroom. I had walked by that section of wall a hundred times already, and there had never been a door there. Besides, the library was missing, too.

The truth of the matter was that the whole ordeal was really unsettling. I suddenly found myself frightened to be in the home. But what else could I do? Where could I go? If I talked to anyone about the room, they would think I was insane.

A thought occurred to me. Perhaps it was a haunted house, if such things existed. I did believe in the paranormal. It's just that I'd never experienced it before. Maybe I could find someone who knew the history of the place. I could get some information on the house. If there were stories about weird things happening, someone would know. I could ask general questions, and wouldn't have to say anything specific.

That was a good plan, and I felt somewhat better. I was awfully shaken, but managed to shower and get dressed, and then make a piece of toast and jam in the kitchen. The only problem with my plan was that I had no idea who I could ask.

I thought a good place to start would be the local library. Small town libraries always had some old newspapers, or slim books written by local historians. At least, it was as good a place as any to start.

I snatched up my handbag and was in such a rush to leave the house that was now making me feel so uneasy, that I didn't notice the mail woman right by my front door. Later, I would realise how odd it was for the woman to be up by the door, considering the mailbox was at the front gate of the house, but when it happened, I simply felt bad about hitting the woman with the door.

"Watch it!" the mail woman yelled as she staggered to the side, placing a hand on the veranda post to keep herself from being bowled over.

"I'm sorry!" I said, hurrying to seize the woman's arm to steady her.

"Let go!" the woman said, jerking her arm from my grasp.

I was a little shocked at how angry the woman seemed. I looked her over. She was wearing baggy grey shorts and a blue shirt, and over her arm was a grey mail bag. Her hair was wildly curly and cut to just above her shoulders, and the woman was what I would call chunky, a little more weight on her frame than she needed.

"Sorry, it was an accident," I said quickly.

"Well, that doesn't keep me from getting knocked over, does it?" she snapped.

I had heard enough from the woman to know I didn't like her. She was just so rude and angry.

"I understand that, but it was an accident and I'm sorry."

"Yes, I heard you the first time," the woman said. "Do you live here now?"

"Yes," I said. "I'm Amelia."

The woman broke into a grin. "Kayleen," she said. "I'm the mail lady."

"Nice to meet you," I lied, wondering how much a ten foot fence with spikes on the top and an electronically locked gate would cost.

"Mail's in the box," Kayleen said, hitching a fat thumb over her shoulder. And then she turned and took a short cut across the flowers, leaving a trail of crushed pansies in her wake.

I watched her go before I moved down to the mailbox and pulled open the little door. Inside were a few envelopes, all of them marked with my aunt's name. Oh dear. I would have to return them to sender, along with a note that my aunt had died, or "crossed over" as the locals seemed to call it. I took the envelopes with me to my car, and climbed behind the wheel.

I drove to town, hoping I would find the town library easily enough. As I drove, I tried to convince myself that I had simply missed the room. The door had been there the whole time, but I had just missed it. And perhaps I'd had too much wine last night, and had missed the library room as well. It was certainly the most believable explanation, although it just wasn't one I could buy. I just couldn't sell my own mind on the fact that I had walked by a door so many times and had never registered it, or that the library room had vanished.

Thinking about the fact that there was simply no way for that room to exist or the library room to vanish made me squirm in my seat. I was frightened, and growing more scared by the minute.

I finally found the library down a side street. To my relief, it had an 'Open' sign outside. I parked the car and hurried inside. It was a small place with a long counter to the right, and shelves of books along with tables and chairs to the left. There was a tall, older woman behind the counter, and I tried there first.

"Can I help you?" the woman asked.

I smiled politely, and pressed my hands against my sides to stop them trembling. "I'm new in town. I just moved in, and I was wondering if I could find some information about the town," I asked. I could hardly tell her that my house was growing rooms that shouldn't be there and deleting other rooms.

"Yes, we have the historical society here," the woman said. She had a name tag which read 'Marilyn.' "But you might just want to go talk to Joe."

"Who's Joe?" I asked.

Marilyn smiled. "He's the local historian, so to speak. He knows everything about this town. You're in luck. He's in the back right now doing some research." She pointed to a door at the back of the room.

"Thanks," I said, and walked over the door.

I knocked on the door, and then poked my head around it. "I'm looking for Joe," I said.

An elderly man looked up. "That's me," he said. "What can I help you with?

I walked over to his desk. He was surrounded by old, yellowing sheets of parchment. I looked at the closest one. It had the words, 'Certificate of Title' with 'New South Wales' written below in a flowery font. Next to that were the words, 'Cancelled. See Auto Folio.' It was dated February 4, 1902.

"Wow," I said. "What a lovely old document."

Joe appeared pleased by my words. "Local history is fascinating," he said.

I nodded, and realised I hadn't answered his question. "I'm Amelia Spelled," I said. "My Aunt Angelica recently died and left me her house in Salisbury Street."

"Oh, yes," Joe said. "I was sorry to hear about your aunt. You must want to ask about her house. Well, I guess it's your house now." He stood up, and crossed to some ancient, grey filing cabinets. He pulled one open and rummaged around in it for a while before producing a document, which he handed to me.

I looked down at the document. The first paragraph said, "This is an original colonial style late

1880s timber house with Arts and Crafts style gable added in the centre of the earlier street elevation. It is the steep slope of the barge boards over a flying decorative gable, designed to intersect with the original veranda eaves lines, that leaves a striking impression of the building."

This was all very interesting, but how was I going to segue to matters of moving rooms?

"I can make you a photocopy of this," Joe offered.

"Thanks, that would be great," I said. "By the way, have you ever heard that it's haunted, or anything like that?"

Joe looked at me strangely. "Have you heard stories of strange events?" he asked, narrowing his eyes.

I nodded. "Yes." It was either that or say that I'd experienced it for myself.

"Oh, you're asking if there's some sort of story? A woman died there or some such thing, and now she haunts the house? No, there's nothing like that, not to my knowledge, and I don't mind telling you that I know a lot about that house, and every other house in town. There's no big tragedy or scary story. Well, people have just claimed to see people, figures, walking on the lawn, peeking out of windows, but that's the case with most of the older houses in this town."

I nodded, disappointed that I had drawn a blank.

"Of course, there were the robbers," Joe said.

"Robbers?" I asked.

Joe shrugged. "The robbers must've been on drugs. Two men broke into that house, some years ago," he continued with a chuckle. "They were going to rob the place, and they came running out hours later. They turned themselves in. They said the house had trapped them, that they couldn't find their way out of the house. They said that rooms appeared that never existed before. It scared them straight. I bet they never tried to rob a house again." He laughed.

My mouth fell open, and I tried to cover the fact that I was shocked. "Are they the only stories about the house?" I asked.

Joe nodded thoughtfully, his finger on his chin. "Well, there are rumours of all kinds of strange things happening in that house. And I suppose you've heard the rumour that your aunt was a witch?"

"A witch?" I screeched. "A witch?"

Joe looked surprised by my reaction. "I'm sorry.

I didn't realise that you hadn't heard. Of course, there's no such thing as witches, or ghosts for that matter. Don't let it trouble you. Small country towns are full of idle gossip. Everyone knows everyone else's business, and what they don't know, they make up."

I forced a smile onto my lips, but the words that were coming out of Joe's mouth were making me uneasy.

I was not the first person to experience the moving rooms in the house.

My aunt was a witch.

What had I gotten myself into? I thought I was going to pass out.

CHAPTER 12

I lingered in the parking lot as I stared at the cake store. It was way too early in the morning to be dealing with eggs and milk and other flammable objects. I definitely needed to get some practice in before opening time, especially while business was slow.

Indeed, business was worriedly slow. Sure, the house and store were fully paid for, but there were still utilities and food to think about. Rumours were spreading around town like wildfire that Brant McCallum died after eating the cake. Never mind that the police had said otherwise. Until the cause of McCallum's death was found, people were going to assume it was from the cake he ate, right here in the cake shop. It was human nature.

I took a deep breath and tried to think of the

bright side. There was no rent. My picture wasn't in the papers over McCallum's death. I even had Thyme to help me get on my feet. Things would work out eventually, right?

Still, the shop used to have two staff members, my aunt and Thyme. Now there was only Thyme. At some point, I would have to pull my weight and learn how to bake.

I made my way to the back door. First things first. I needed to wipe down everything, mop and clean. After all, the last thing I needed was an off-chance customer coming in and seeing a glass counter covered in fingerprints or something. No need to become known as the messy cake shop where someone died.

To my surprise, I found the door unlocked. Had I forgotten to lock it the night before? No, I was pretty sure I had locked it. I was paranoid like that, especially with the big-city neighbourhood I had lived in not so long before. Thyme had a set of keys, but I hadn't asked Thyme to open early today.

I thought about calling the authorities to check it out just in case. It would probably be the most logical thing to do. Then I thought again, and realised that was the last thing I'd need. A man dies, and then the police come days later? No, I'd never get this place running. People would avoid it like the plague.

I carefully opened the door and peeked in. If there was nothing amiss, there wouldn't be a reason to raise a fuss. I would just do a good check and then have the locks changed or something. I should have done that on day one anyway. There's no telling how many of Angelica's old helpers were out there with a copy of the key.

Suddenly every hair on the back of my neck stood on end. Everything looked just the way I had left it the day before. I didn't see a mess or any signs of being pilfered. There was even a pleasing scent of spices and sugar wafting in the air. It reminded me of the spice cake I had tried to bake the day the fire department came by. Yet there was a sound that definitely did not fit in. There was a soft voice whispering something in a flickering light just out of my sight. I didn't recognise the words, but at the same time there was an odd familiarity about it.

I carefully peered around the door to the kitchen. To my surprise, I saw Thyme standing at a counter. She looked normal enough, wearing slacks and an embroidered blouse. Her features looked vague in the early sunlight and the flickering candle in front of her. A candle! Why were the lights out?

Ruprecht, as executor of my aunt's will, had assured me the bills were taken care of for this month. Surely I shouldn't have a problem there?

Thyme was staring at the candle in deep concentration, chanting something as she seemed completely engrossed in the flame. Her right hand slowly moved around the flickering candle as she sprinkled some sort of powder around it in a circle. What in the world was she doing?

"Hey, Thyme," I said as I opened the door.

Thyme jumped back with a start, spilling everything into a haphazard mess on the counter.

"Oh! I didn't expect to see you so early." Thyme was clearly flustered as she snuffed the candle and tried to hide the mess behind her back. "I thought you said you were coming at the usual time today?"

"I thought I would start getting used to the place," I explained as I studied the mess on the counter.

"You really startled me. I thought you'd broken in. Serves me right for not locking the door behind me, huh?" Thyme's conversational tone seemed a little strained as she reached for an odd iron bowl I had never seen before.

"Sorry," I said. It wasn't like Thyme to be so skittish. Nothing about the stuff on the countertop made any sense to me, either. "Um, what about you? What's all this first thing in the morning?"

"Oh. It's just, you know, a spice mix," Thyme said with an apologetic smile. "I was going to clean it right up. Experts say that filling a place with kitchen smells makes it more welcoming. It's good energy. We need welcoming, right?"

I could not argue with that part. But still, that didn't explain what she was doing. "What's with the candle and chanting thing?"

"Good luck?" Thyme responded in an oddly questioning tone. She looked, well, worried wasn't the right word. Anxious? No, I couldn't quite put my finger on the word. Something had made her quite uncomfortable, though. It was obvious by the way she was acting.

"Oh, the others are going to be so mad at me." She sighed in resignation as she waved her hand in an anticlockwise motion over the scattered mess. "It was a spell. Just a little one."

I was taken off guard. What was all this about spells and energy and stuff? "Thyme, please slow down and tell me exactly what's going on."

Thyme winced as she held the odd bowl in her hands and studied me. "I'm in so much trouble."

~

A FEW MINUTES LATER, Thyme was leading me the few doors down to Ruprecht Foxtin-Flynn's shop. I didn't know what to make of it. I tried to ask her several times, but she just kept saying that Ruprecht was better at answering these kinds of questions than she was.

I had been preoccupied the last time I had been in here. It was an amazingly quaint little shop. It looked like something out of a story book. Antiques and stacks of books were scattered everywhere. There were desks and tables of solid wood, and the atmosphere was decidedly quirky. Yet I didn't see any talking owls or crystal balls, and definitely no brooms or giant cauldrons. There was nothing to suggest that Ruprecht would have any idea what this stuff was about.

Ruprecht was waiting for us with a kindly smile on his face. His knobbly fingers were interlaced in front of him as he regarded the two of us. As always, his cats were watching us with keen interest. "Welcome, ladies. May I offer you both some tea? I didn't expect this conversation to happen for quite some time," he said, as he turned towards his back office.

"Sorry about that," Thyme said sheepishly. "I was careless. I just wanted to help."

"Always with the best of intentions, my dear," Ruprecht replied as he paused in his trek and shook his hand, waving off the apology. "All things happen with a purpose."

I watched the interaction, not having a clue what was going on. I consoled myself with the fact that I was about to find out. I looked around the room, and then at the cats as they watched me with their amber eyes from which shone an almost human-like intelligence. No, that was silly. Thyme's weird ramblings were infectious. "I think I'm misunderstanding something here, Ruprecht," I said. "Thyme was saying something about a spell and energy. Well, I had trouble following it, to tell the truth."

"All in good time, my dear. There's no need to rush," Ruprecht responded.

"I AM A WHAT?" I demanded as I nearly dropped my tea.

"A witch," Thyme replied cheerfully before taking a generous sip of her tea. She seemed to recover her usual cheerful demeanour as soon as Ruprecht took over explaining the situation.

Ruprecht cleared his throat and gave Thyme a stern look, which was met with a small apologetic smile. The older man looked back over to me. "Yes. You have inherited the legacy of your father and aunt. Your father, of course, rejected that part of himself. And, naturally, we respected that decision. It was always Angelica's hope that you would eventually grow to embrace your heritage. Our bloodlines have dwindled over the past few generations. Heirs tend to be a precious few."

I gasped. "My mother was head of the women's mission group! There's no way she was married to a witch."

Thyme sighed and shook her head. "It's like being better at science, or a faster runner. It's just something you are born with."

"Do you mean Wicca?" I had heard of Wicca.

Thyme shook her head again. "No, we're traditional witches. Wicca is a specific modern religion, started by Gerard Gardiner in 1954."

I gave a short laugh and looked between them as I tried to process this. Of course. This was some sort of elaborate prank, a way to poke fun at the new outsider. They must have known I would hear the town rumour that Aunt Angelica was a witch, and thought they'd have some fun with it. An uncle on Dad's side used to take guests from the city snipe-hunting, an old prank that left the outsider hunched over with a burlap bag for hours, and walking home on their own after they figured out snipes don't exist. Internet searches finally took all the fun out of it for him.

But really. "A witch? Like hocus pocus and flying on broomsticks? Turning ex-boyfriends into frogs?" *Well, that's a thought, anyway*, I added silently.

Thyme laughed, "No, no, no. You watch too much TV. That's the Hollywood version of witches. No flying. No shape shifting. It's all pretty dull in comparison, I guess."

Ruprecht regarded me over his glasses. "All things are bound together by energy. Witches are simply those who are more sensitive to that energy. It can be enhanced, re-channelled, manipulated. Changed by the force of will, within limits, naturally."

"Kind of like cooking." Thyme tapped a slender finger on the table thoughtfully. "Most creative people have some level of witch in them. They take the abstract energy and shape it into a physical form. They are usually crafters, writers, artists, musicians. They all find an outlet to create things. We do that too, mostly with potions and herbs, teas, stuff like that."

I immediately looked down suspiciously at the cup of tea in my hands and set it down. "Well, that settles it. I have zilch talent making anything. I can't even make toast without setting off a fire alarm."

"On the contrary, my dear." Ruprecht watched me with that same patient smile. "It is proof of your talent, quite a lot of untapped potential at that."

"Right." I was talented, and my lack of talent proved it, right. That made sense, not! My head was spinning.

"You've been through a rough time," Thyme said soothingly. "You haven't had anyone to rely on in years, so I bet you had to be a big girl and deal with it, right? But those feelings have to go somewhere. So, given you won't let them out normally, they go straight into whatever you make. Namely food."

"You're an Aries," Ruprecht said. "Your element is fire and you have a natural affinity with flame. Candle magick will be your forte, once you learn to control your powers."

"Powers?" I echoed.

Ruprecht reached out to pat my hand gently.

"Perhaps best to call it 'energies.' Don't fret. Angelica made sure you would be among friends: myself and Thyme, my granddaughter, and Camino. We will all do what we can to help you learn. You won't be left to learn your heritage on your own."

I frowned and stood up. This was too much, even for a prank. These people acted like they really believed what they were saying. They were completely delusional. "I need to get back to work."

"I'll go with you," Thyme said.

Ruprecht rose slowly and gave me a kind smile. "Very well, my dear. Please come by any time you have questions for us. You no longer need to walk these paths alone."

I managed a half hearted nod before rushing out, pointedly ignoring the scrutinising gazes of the cats on my way out. None of it was real. My father hadn't been some witch. I wasn't a witch. People don't make potions and cast spells.

CHAPTER 13

I was busy behind the front counter, practicing putting icing on cupcakes. I found I was improving at that, given that no flames were involved, and it was something I could do to help while Thyme was out in the kitchen baking.

The door chimed as it was pushed open. I turned my attention to my new customer and my heart caught in my throat when I saw it was Craig.

He smiled as he stopped in front of the counter. "I messed you up," he said, tilting his head at the icing.

"No, just practicing," I said. "Believe me, there's nothing special to mess up."

"Hey, it looked better than I could do," Craig said.

"So, what can I get for you?" I asked, hoping

my cheeks were not bright red. They sure felt hot at the sight of Craig.

"I was wondering if you still made cupcakes," Craig said. "Like your aunt did."

I laughed and tapped the top of the counter. Under the countertop was the glass case, inside which were numerous cupcakes in various flavours.

"Oh, wow," he said. "I'm not sure how I missed that."

"It's all right. Hey, buy fifty if you want to. I think Thyme needs to stop making so many in the morning."

"Let me get a chocolate cake with buttercream icing please. Yeah, the blue icing there," Craig said, pointing to the one he wanted.

I placed the cupcake inside a small box. "Four fifty," I said as I slid the box across the countertop.

Craig handed over five dollars in cash and dumped the fifty cents change into the small glass jar that read 'Tips.' "Business not going well?" he asked as he opened the box and pulled out the cupcake. He took a bite. "Wow, this is amazing," he said.

"No, business is horrible," I admitted.

Craig frowned. "It takes a little while for some

of the people here to warm up to newcomers. We don't get a lot of newcomers in Bayberry Creek."

"I think it might have something more to do with the death in here the other day."

"Well, it wasn't your fault, was it?"

"No!" I exclaimed. "The police said it was natural causes. They tested all the cake samples and the results were all clear."

"Well, I'm sure everyone else knows that."

I shook my head. "That's not what I've heard. Brant McCallum died right after eating a cake sample for his wedding, the poor guy."

Craig popped the last of the cupcake into his mouth. "So, what do you think happened to Brant? What did the cops mean by natural causes?"

"I don't know exactly," I admitted. "That's all they said. Natural causes, his heart, although they said he didn't have a heart condition. But I'll tell you one thing, it didn't seem natural to me. It seemed pretty unnatural."

"What do you mean?" Craig asked. He leant forward, against the counter.

"He took a bite, and it just, well, I know it makes it sound like it was the cakes here, and it wasn't. He took a bite and his eyes just went big, like he knew something was wrong."

Craig rubbed his chin. "Maybe it was a heart attack, after all. Maybe he felt it, and maybe him biting into your cake didn't mean anything. It was just a coincidence."

"I don't know," I said with a shrug. "That's a pretty big coincidence."

"But what are you saying?" Craig asked. "What do you think happened?"

I shrugged again. "I don't know. I just know that it wasn't a heart attack. I would bet anything."

"Do you think someone killed him?"

"Maybe."

"Well, if you could prove that, people would know someone actually murdered Brant, and that it wasn't your cake. That would save your business."

I smiled. It was sweet of Craig to be so helpful. "But how am I supposed to prove it? That's a job for the police."

Craig shook his head. "It doesn't sound as though they're going to be looking into it much, does it? Natural causes, case closed."

"Yeah, but I'm not a cop, or a detective." I pulled a face. "I don't know how to solve a crime."

Craig laughed and nodded. "You have a point there."

"I wouldn't even know where to start," I said.

"Hey, it was just an idea," Craig said. "Something to help. But it's crazy, so forget I said anything."

But I couldn't forget that he had said anything. He left shortly after that, but I couldn't recall any more of our conversation. My mind was too preoccupied. I needed to make sure that business picked up again. Aunt Angelica had left the cake store to me, and I couldn't let her down. I needed to find out what had happened to Brant McCallum. If I could somehow prove he was murdered, then the locals wouldn't be suspicious of the cake store anymore, and everything my aunt had worked so hard to achieve wouldn't be flushed down the drain.

The rest of the day passed slowly, but when it was time to close up, I did so quickly. I knew exactly what I needed to do. I hurried to my car and drove home. I spent a half hour or so browsing, and then I downloaded a stack of books to my iPad. They all had to do with forensics and crime solving.

I read late into the night, and the oddness of the new room almost didn't matter at all, nor did the fact that I was surrounded by witches, or so they said. I read first on the couch, eating a quick dinner that had been prepared in the microwave, what else! When my eyes were tired and my back and neck were sore, I took the iPad to my bedroom, and kept reading.

I was awoken by the iPad crashing onto my head. It hurt quite a bit. I suppose that was one of the drawbacks of reading on an iPad rather than reading a 'real' book, as people like to call them. If you fall asleep and a book falls on your head, it doesn't hurt, but an iPad really hurts, trust me.

Anyway, what was I thinking? The books on forensics and crime solving were interesting. Well, some of them were—others were as dry as dust—but I couldn't see how they helped inexperienced sleuths like I was. I needed help.

CHAPTER 14

One thing was certain. I had to solve the murder of Brant McCallum to clear the cloud of suspicion that hung over the cake store. It was the only way I could regain the trust of Aunt Angelica's customers. I had pointed that out to Thyme who was in full agreement. She suggested we speak to Ruprecht.

I felt a little strange speaking to Ruprecht after the whole 'your-aunt-was-a-witch,' 'your-father-was-a-witch,' 'you-are-a-witch thing.' While I didn't accept that I was a witch, I had spent a lot of time on YouTube, and I had a better understanding of the whole witch thing now.

Mint stood in the doorway to *Glinda's* with a broad smile across her face. "Grandfather's expecting you." She led us to the back room.

Ruprecht was sitting by a table with a large teapot of hot tea, four empty bone china mugs (at least I hoped they were bone china, and not bone), and the same type of cakes he had offered me last time. He gripped the pot in his right hand and poured tea into each of the mugs. Steam swirled from each as the warm liquid reached their brims. He didn't say a single word as he did this, but when he was done, he returned the teapot to its original location and then sipped from the cup before him. After he placed it back down, he looked up at us. "So, what brings you here?" he asked in a gentle tone.

I was sure that he already knew why we had come, but I decided to answer anyway. "I need your help. Business has dropped right off, and we've heard rumours around town that Brant McCallum died from eating our cake. I'm sure business will pick up again if we could find out what really happened to him. Who would have wanted to kill that man?"

Ruprecht leant forward in his chair and took another sip from his cup. "Well, I believe even those with the most trivial of motives could still be the number one suspect. Brant was not well liked by any means. Perhaps there were people who respected him, but mostly he was loathed." He tapped his chin. "Perhaps we can brainstorm and think up a list of suspects."

"That's what we were hoping," Thyme said, giving me an encouraging nod, "but where do we start?"

Ruprecht sat back in his chair and looked up at the high ceiling. I wasn't sure what he was thinking, but I hoped his thoughts, whatever they were, would throw some light on my problem. Finally he spoke. "We must start with those who had an obvious problem with the man. We must bring to mind any old altercations, any recent disputes, or anything else that could give someone a reason to murder the man."

Mint sat forward and spoke. "The first person who comes to my mind is Dermott Smith. Just a few weeks ago, there was a huge dispute over a big poker tournament that came to town. Smith and Brant McCallum made it into the final round, and of course, Brant won somehow. I'm not sure what the actual sum involved was, but Dermott was very upset soon afterwards. He said that he'd been cheated and that McCallum had been counting cards during their match."

I sat in silence for several minutes, taking it all

in. Was being cheated in a poker game truly reason enough to murder someone?

"Do you think Dermott Smith is a calculating killer? Whoever pulled this off knew what they were doing. If it was poison—and really, what else could it have been?—it was given in advance, as he didn't ingest any poison in the cake store. To me, it sounds more like Bill Gafney could have his hands in this mess." Thyme picked up one of the cakes as she finished her sentence. She took a big bite from it and then washed it down with a sip of tea. "He's running for mayor, and rumour has it that Brant had some dirt on him. That sounds like as good a reason as any to want someone killed," she explained.

I sighed. I now had the names of two suspects, two names circling around in my mind, but which was the more likely culprit: the man who had lost a poker game, or the politician who had everything to lose if Brant opened his mouth?

"Gafney is known around town as someone who can't be trusted with his own secrets, let alone anyone else's. Do you really think he would be able to pull off something like this without a single person knowing about it?" Ruprecht paused after speaking, and then looked directly at me. "Either of these men could be the killer, but I think there's still at least one person we haven't mentioned yet. I believe there's someone who might have a larger stake in all of this, someone who might have known where Brant would be at the very day and time of his death."

I sat up, listening intently as I waited to hear the name of another possible suspect. "Who would have known Brant would be at my shop at that time? Was that killer trying to frame me, or was the entire cake thing just a coincidence?"

Ruprecht finished his tea and gently slid his cup back onto the table. He looked at each of us. "A local delivery driver named Jason Mackay has been very vocal about his feelings towards McCallum. Since he typically drops off any deliveries for me shortly after dealing with Brant, I've spoken to him on several occasions about it."

Mint seemed puzzled. "You really think Jason had something to do with this?" she asked.

"Jason Mackay had some trouble with his previous delivery van, so he was looking for a reliable replacement. After all, a delivery man's truck is his everything, much like cakes are yours now, and books and antiques are ours," Ruprecht said, looking at each of us as he spoke about us. "The truck turned out to have serious faults, which Jason believes Brant knew about all the while. He believes he purposefully sold him an unreliable vehicle."

"A broken down van?" I asked. "You think someone murdered a man over being sold a lemon?"

Ruprecht shook his head. "No, I think someone might have wanted to kill over what that broken down truck caused. Without a reliable vehicle to transport goods, Mackay lost his business. That led to a foreclosure on his home, and ultimately, it all caused his wife to leave him." He refilled his cup from the delicate green and pink teapot. After taking a sip, he looked at Thyme, and then shifted his focus back to me. "I do believe one of these suspects might be our culprit, but there must be other suspects that we haven't as yet considered."

"Well, I think all three had motives and maybe even opportunity," Thyme said. "Either way though, I think we need to investigate all three of them. Gafney is still my pick, but only because he's the only one of the three that I'm okay with calling a criminal at this point."

Mint shifted in her chair. She glanced over at me and spoke softly. "I think Thyme could be right, but that being said, I believe that Dermott is the offender. I've seen him very angry, and he's the only man who's ever sent chills down my spine, aside from Brant himself."

We all sat in silence for the next few minutes, but Ruprecht finally spoke up. "Bill Gafney and Dermott Smith are both men I fail to trust. Jason, however, makes me apprehensive. Regardless, if any of us think we know who killed Brant right now, we are likely mistaken. I think Thyme and Mint are both correct in saying that we need to know more about these men before deciding which of them is the villain. All we can offer now is speculation, and we need much more than that."

"So what do we do now?" I asked.

Ruprecht pulled himself to his feet and wandered over to one of the old bookshelves that lined the wall. I watched as he placed a single finger on each book until he touched a specific one and didn't move onto the next. He slid that book into his other hand and then opened it up. I studied him as he stood in silence, apparently reading from the old tome. He clapped the book shut and then spoke once more. "We should try to discount each of these suspects, one by one."

Mint nodded. "Yes! We could try to lure all three men to Amelia's home under some sort of pretence, like a party or something. That way we can let the house narrow down which of them is the murderer," she said.

My face twisted with confusion. "Excuse me?"

Ruprecht walked back over and sat down. "There's something about your new home that you should probably be aware of."

I nodded. "Oh, you mean the changing rooms? I found that out for myself! So I'm not going mad? What a relief!" The words all tumbled out one after the other, and then I put my head between my hands. I took a deep breath and continued babbling. "First the library was there, then it was a bedroom, and then I woke up in a room that doesn't exist, but it does now…" My voice trailed away as Thyme and Mint exchanged worried glances.

"Why didn't you tell me?" Thyme asked.

"'Cause you'd think I was mad!" I said.

Ruprecht rubbed his forehead, and when he spoke, his tone was solemn. "I'm sorry we didn't tell you, Amelia, but you wouldn't have believed us, if you didn't see it for yourself. If only you had known Angelica. She would've explained everything. I didn't think the house would change on you so soon. It's only ever changed rooms before in the presence of experienced witches."

I would have been flattered if I didn't feel that I was barely hanging on to my last vestiges of sanity.

Ruprecht did not appear to notice my state, for he continued. "Now I must tell you that the house has two habits: firstly, it changes rooms in the presence of witches, and secondly, it frightens people it doesn't like."

"It doesn't like?" I repeated with rising hysteria. "Are you saying that the house has its own dislikes?"

Mint and Thyme looked at each other again.

"The way it works is like this," Ruprecht said. "If the house doesn't like someone, the house will respond by closing its walls on its target. The only people who can see this happening however, are the victims." He shot me a worried look and then added, "Well, 'victims' is too strong a word. They are unharmed, just frightened."

"You mean scared to death?" I asked shrilly.

"Actually," Ruprecht continued, "I shouldn't have said the only people who can see it happening are the victims. If the house is really angry, we will see a hint of the walls closing on them, but not in a way that scares us. They, of course, will be terrified."

I clutched at my head, and took a deep breath.

"I think she needs a brandy," Mint said.

Thyme leaped to her feet and reached for an old, crystal cut glass bottle. She poured me a drink of the amber liquid. I snatched it and downed it in one go. My throat burned, and my eyes streamed. "What on earth was that?" I spluttered between coughs.

"Brandy, I hope. Right?" Thyme looked hopefully at Ruprecht, who responded with something half way between a nod and a shrug.

My concerns about the house were now secondary to the awful scalding feeling in my throat. I was a wine person. I'd never had anything stronger than a dry white. "So you're saying my house can just crush people with its walls if it doesn't like them?" My voice seemed to come from far away, and was that two of Ruprecht I could see?

"No, it's simply a scare tactic," Thyme said, "but it will help us figure out which of the three men is the killer. The house should scare one of them and not the others." She laughed, and I started to giggle. In fact, I couldn't stop giggling.

Ruprecht, both of him, appeared to be speaking. "Yes, I believe our best bet will be to invite the three men to your home for what we'll call a welcoming party. I'll also invite a few of my own customers to make up the guest numbers."

"Does that mean I have to cook?" I asked between giggles.

"No," Thyme said solemnly. "It's a party, not a witch burning."

CHAPTER 15

*M*int had given me a ride home, and when she left me at the front gate, I assured her that I was fine. I walked somewhat unevenly up the front path and managed to unlock the front door, and then turned to wave to Mint.

"Are you sure you're all right?" she yelled through the car window.

I waved in affirmation, and then shut the door behind me. I didn't feel too well, so went to the bathroom and splashed water on my face. I was light headed and dizzy. "I need some fresh air," I said to Willow and Hawthorn, who sat looking at me, their heads on the side. "I'll go for a nice walk around town. I think I've had too much to drink." My speech sounded slurred, even to me.

The evening air was cooling, a fact that I noted,

but did not register enough to take a coat. I had more trouble going down the front steps than I'd had going up them moments earlier. I sat on the bottom step and took a few deep breaths. The moon was rising in the east. It was full, and looked enormous coming over the horizon. I squinted and tried to focus my eyes.

I felt a little queasy, but nevertheless set off at a wobbly walk. I wouldn't have liked to walk in the city after dark, not in the neighbourhood where I'd lived, but everyone said that Bayberry Creek was a safe town. Most people didn't even lock their doors. *The town wasn't safe for Brant McCallum*, I thought, and I shivered.

I walked on and on, aimlessly. I didn't feel any better, but then again, I didn't feel any worse. I soon found myself in a more deserted part of town, right on its edge. Suburban rows of houses gave way to five acre lots, with the houses set well back from the road.

I now wasn't sure where I was. I turned around and tried to head back to my house, but I wasn't sure of the direction to go. It was darker away from the streetlights, and that didn't help. I came to a football field, and cut across it.

There were thick trees on the other side of the

football field, and they glowed with the lights of the town behind. I figured I must be heading in the right direction. I rounded a tree and saw a tall figure in front of me.

I froze with fear. I fought against the waves of blind panic that threatened to engulf me. The figure moved towards me. I was too scared to run, so leant back against the tree, my hands behind me for support.

"I'm sorry if I scared you," a man's voice said. "Are you lost?"

I was too frightened to speak, so I nodded. My breath was coming in short bursts.

The figure stepped closer to me and I cowered.

"Hi," the tall man said. "I'm Alder Vervain. I've seen you around town. Amelia Spelled, right?"

"Yes," I said, having finally found my voice. Someone who intended me harm would hardly introduce himself.

He stepped into the light, and a wave of fear washed over me once more. This was the man I had seen watching me at Angelica's funeral, the same man I'd overheard Camino telling the others was parked in his car near my house one evening. Nevertheless, there was nothing threatening in his manner. "I'll take you home," he said.

I looked him up and down. *Wow, he's gorgeous*, I thought.

Alder chuckled. "Thanks. Have you been drinking?"

Oops, did I say that aloud? I wondered.

"Yes," he said with a smile.

I rubbed my head. That brandy must've been strong. I was saying things that I thought I was thinking. How embarrassing. "Ruprecht—or was it Thyme?—gave me some brandy and I drank it all in one go," I babbled. "I feel a bit weird. I'm not much used to strong drink."

He smiled again. "Obviously. Let's get you home. You shouldn't be out after dark."

"Everyone says this is a safe town," I protested.

"It most likely is," he said, "but you should keep to the houses and the street lights. This is just out of town."

I shivered, and he immediately took off his coat and draped it around my shoulders. His coat smelled smoky and sweet, of cedar and lime soap, masculine and attractive. I pulled it closely around me.

What was I thinking? Was I simply attracted to his overt masculinity? I was attracted to Craig, not to this stranger. Just then, I stumbled down the edge of the sloping road, and Alder caught my arm. He pulled me to him in an attempt to keep me on my feet. I was facing him; his arms were around me. At that moment, I wanted nothing more than for him to kiss me, and for an instant I thought he was going to. I raised my lips to his, just as his arms tightened around me, but then he pulled away.

I was mortified. I was lucky it was dark, as I was sure my face was bright red. Alder placed his hand under my elbow to guide me. His touch sent electric tingles down my body. I wanted nothing more than to kiss him, and be against his muscular body once more.

What was wrong with me? If this was how I acted when I'd had too much to drink, I'd have to be careful from now on. Back to wine for me.

By the time we reached Salisbury Street, I felt almost back to normal. I expected that Alder would walk me to my door, so I was surprised when he stopped a few houses down. "I'll wait here," he said, releasing my elbow, much to my disappointment. "I'll watch until you get safely inside."

Was he afraid Camino would see him? Why didn't he walk me to my door? I thanked him, and left, but with many questions that I suspected would be answered none too soon. I walked up my path, welcomed by the fragrance of the French lavenders and the buddleia trees, and perhaps, even the house itself.

As I fell into bed, ignoring the disapproving looks of Willow and Hawthorn, I realised that Alder's coat was still around my shoulders. I smiled and snuggled into it as I fell asleep.

CHAPTER 16

hyme and I worked to prepare the house for our guests. As it was spring, we were going to have the party out in the garden. Thyme had told me that the house could possibly take a dislike to anyone, and while the chances were remote that it would do so, we couldn't risk it happening. At the same time, we had to lure the three murder suspects into the house. Apparently it was a given that the house would react violently to anyone who had committed murder.

I was growing somewhat accustomed to having a weird house. I was even growing accustomed to being a witch, although I still wasn't sure what witchcraft actually involved.

I had not seen Alder since that night, and so had no opportunity to return his coat. I had been hoping he would come to fetch it. I did not like to ask the others where he lived, because they had spoken of him with mistrust. I was also somewhat embarrassed by my behaviour that night.

Hawthorn ran over to me and purred. "What do you want now?" I said. "I've already fed you." Willow immediately sat up from his perch on the windowsill and tilted his head, looking at me intensely. He then shot off towards the floor and ran right through my legs. I turned to see his tail disappear quickly around a corner. When I looked back at Hawthorn, I saw she hadn't moved an inch.

Just as I switched the vacuum back on, Thyme walked out from the kitchen.

"How's the food coming along?" I asked her, after I switched it off again.

She smiled. "It's all going well. Ruprecht and Mint are outside with the first of the guests."

Something occurred to me. "I know we want to keep them all out of the house, but what happens if they want to use the bathroom?"

"That's fine," Thyme said. "They can use the small powder room at the back of the house. I don't think the house will mind that, even if the house doesn't like them."

"Great, that's a relief," I said, and then I

realised I was talking about the house like I'd talk about a person. Oh well, that's what Thyme and the others were doing. I shrugged.

"I hope you don't mind that we said you shouldn't invite Craig," Thyme said. "Like we said, it wouldn't be good if he saw a man running out of the house insisting that the house tried to crush him, what with him being your future boyfriend and all." She laughed and gave me playful dig in the ribs.

I hurried to reassure her. "No, that's fine." How did I feel about Craig? He was good looking and nice, but I had never been overwhelmed with the urge to kiss him. Perhaps that was simply because I hadn't had a brandy shot first.

Ruprecht poked his head around the door. "Let's go and meet your guests."

We walked to the front of the house, where everyone was gathered and engaged in conversation. I didn't really know many of the guests, not by name anyway. Thyme was passing around platters of food. As she passed us, she whispered, "Let's see if we can separate the suspects and get them into the house."

I nodded, and followed Ruprecht as he made his way to a tall, slender man with short black hair.

"Amelia, this is a customer of mine. Have you met Jason Mackay before?" he asked me, nodding towards the man.

"No, I haven't," I replied, shaking Jason's hand. "Welcome to my home."

"Oh, thank you," the man replied in a gentle tone. He held a glass of wine in one hand and sipped from it happily. "So, how do you like the town?"

"It's great," I said. "Would you like to look inside the house? Ruprecht could give you the tour."

"Thanks," Jason said. I couldn't tell if he really wanted to look inside the house or not, but he followed Ruprecht nonetheless. One down, two to go.

I took Thyme's arm as she swept by with a food platter. "Okay, so Ruprecht is going to take Jason into the living room. Mint said she's going to get Dermott Smith to discuss a book with her. We just have to get Bill Gafney in there," I said.

Thyme nodded. "All in good time. Just mingle with the guests and try to act normal."

"I'll try to act as normal as I can," I said.

I was engaged in conversation with an elderly lady, and trying to avert my eyes from Kayleen, the mail lady, who was doing a wild dance. At least, I hoped it was a dance. I hoped she wasn't stripping. She was clutching one of the metal poles that held up the wisteria and gyrating around it. She seemed unconcerned that big blobs of purple wisteria had fallen into her hair.

Just as the elderly lady moved on to speak with someone else, Camino appeared beside me. "Who invited the mail lady?" I asked her.

"No one," Camino said with a growl. "She always invites herself to parties."

I was about to ask Camino if Kayleen usually stripped at parties, and what we could do in the way of damage control if she did, when there was a loud yell. All heads turned to the front door of the house. The door flung open, and Jason rushed out. Well, it actually looked like he had been pushed, and hard.

He tumbled headlong towards the stairs, and then did what looked like an impressive gym roll down them. He landed sprawled, face-first, on the lawn.

Camino and I rushed to him.

"What is going on?" he shrieked as he got to his feet, his eyes bulging.

"What do you mean?" I said in my most innocent tone.

"What do *you* mean, what do *I* mean?" he exclaimed. Gone was his gentle tone. "The walls tried to crush me and the doors were all locked!" he shouted. "What on earth just happened? Why aren't you saying anything?"

I plastered what I hoped was a nonchalant look on my face. "Maybe you had too much to drink. Perhaps you just need some fresh air. Can I call a taxi to drive you home?"

"That's a good idea," Camino said, "but I'll drive you home, Jason. Mustn't drive under the influence, you know. You'll be okay. The fresh air will make you feel brand new. Come on now."

Jason took a deep breath. "Just hurry, please. I don't know what happened in there, but I think something's wrong with me."

Camino took Jason by the arm, and he went with her meekly, clutching at his head.

Thyme ran over and pulled me to the side. "What happened in there?" she asked in a frantic tone. "Why did you bring him outside?"

I shook my head. "I didn't. The house spat him out. My house really is haunted," I said in a strained voice as I tried to rationalise the whole thing.

"No, of course it isn't haunted!" Thyme exclaimed. "It just has a mind of its own."

"Is he going to cause a problem?" I asked Thyme. "Though he does seem to believe that he had too much to drink."

"No worries, everything will be fine." Thyme smiled reassuringly as she stepped away from the window. She seemed awfully relaxed for someone who had just watched a house kick out a guest.

"How can you be sure?" I was not convinced. Getting closed in by a house like that? Suddenly finding himself locked inside? That seemed pretty hard to forget.

"Yeah. Like I said, the house has a mind of its own," Thyme assured me with a wave of her hand. "The house will erase his memory. Many houses do that, but to a far lesser degree."

I was shocked. "You're joking, right?"

Thyme shook her head. "You know that thing where you walk into a room and totally blank out as to why you went in there?"

My jaw fell open. "You don't mean…?"

"Yep. The house's doing. Whenever someone stumbles into something they aren't supposed to, their house will erase their short term memory. Just like that! No matter how important it was a minute ago, it's gone along with whatever else the house is erasing."

"Seriously?" I couldn't even bring myself to be surprised that Thyme nodded earnestly. I wondered if there was any truth to her wild claim. I had always wondered how I could completely forget why I had gone into a room. It never made sense to be after something important, only to find myself stuck wondering what I had been after. I had never imagined it could be the *house's* fault.

Well, it had been a really enlightening day. My head was swimming with names and a blur of faces from the party. My house could pick and choose guests, and make me feel crazy. I didn't know which was stranger. I was surprised that I wasn't running down the driveway with my bag in hand already.

"On the bright side, we have our suspect," Thyme said cheerfully. "That's good, right?"

I nodded in agreement. No matter how unconventional this method was, it seemed to have done the trick. Jason Mackay had been expelled by the house. The house saw him as a threat. Perhaps this whole living house security system wasn't such a bad thing after all. I could learn to get used to it.

"Ladies." Mint peeked around the corner,

waving us over frantically. "Could you join me for a minute?"

"Uh oh." I frowned, wondering what had her in such a state. "Do you think someone saw something?"

"I hope not." Thyme looked worried as we made our way back into the house.

"No kidding." They were the only words I managed to say as I took in the scene in the living room.

"Oh dear." Thyme gripped my arm, her eyes wide with dismay.

"Not good, not good, not good," I stammered.

I looked with alarm at the slowly rippling walls and the shifting ceiling. What was going on? The house got rid of the bad guy, right? Why was it closing in?

I scoured the area, seeing both Dermott Smith and Bill Gafney. Dermott was pouring over the appetisers on the table, inspecting them one by one and setting them back down. Bill, on the other hand, was engrossed with his phone. He didn't even notice the eerie creaking sound as the walls slowly buckled in his direction. I could almost swear that the creaking wood sounded like a low growl.

Ruprecht hurried into the room. "Well, this isn't

good," he fretted as he adjusted his glasses. "If the house gets any more agitated, it's liable to throw out the entire guest list."

"I told you that it hated parties." Thyme tightened her grip on my arm. The house grumbled in obvious irritation as the ceiling sagged in warning.

I bit my bottom lip as I fought off a wave of anxiety.

"We better get them out quick before the house decides to take matters into its own hands," Mint said in a quiet voice.

Just then, Dermott Smith looked up at the slowly moving ceiling and reached up a hand to rub at his eyes. He gazed at the ceiling, and then gazed around at us.

Thyme quickly plastered on a professional smile and made her way across the room. "Dermott, it's getting very stuffy in here. Just going out for some fresh air, were you?"

Dermott gazed between her and the walls as they seemed to inch closer slowly. "Yes, yes, I suppose so. Tell me, do you see anything amiss with the room?"

Thyme feigned innocence as she gazed around the room. "Oh? Whatever do you mean?"

"Nothing," Dermott said quickly, shaking his head. "I must be more tired than I thought."

"Oh, you should go get some rest," Thyme said quickly. "It's so stuffy in here and the wine is quite strong."

"I'm fine. I saw some coffee in the kitchen. I'll just go grab a cup." Dermott's tone was dismissive and he made to push past her. I started forward to offer support, but Mint held me back with a soft shake of her head.

Thyme rested her hand on his forearm. "Don't you have one of those tournament things coming up?"

"Next week, a big game." Dermott looked from the sleeve to Thyme. "Never pegged you for a poker player."

"Oh well, I was curious and thought I might try it out." Thyme was speaking with such fake enthusiasm that even I wasn't buying it. "Does it pay a lot of money?"

Dermott gave a snort. "Isn't a game for amateurs. With the stakes we play for, you'd lose the shirt off your back in the first round."

"Sounds pretty intense." Thyme must have had a lot of practice dealing with customers. I had no idea how she was keeping such a straight face as the man launched into a big story about what a wonderful poker player he was. "It's so stuffy in here," she said. "How about we go outside and you tell me all about it?"

Thankfully, with the prospect of talking about himself, Dermott seemed more open to going back outside. He gave a final concerned glance around the room before making his way out.

"Now for Bill Gafney," Ruprecht said.

CHAPTER 17

*R*uprecht and I hurried back up the steps and onto the veranda. As my hand closed around the old brass doorknob, Mint pulled the door open. "Whoa!" she said, startling me. "Amelia! Grandfather! I'm so sorry. We were just looking for you. I think I found the guilty man."

I pulled a face. "What? But the house just closed in on Jason Mackay as well as Dermott Smith."

Mint shook her head. "Weird. Well I'm having trouble with Bill Gafney. The walls are buckling around him. He hasn't noticed yet though, but I can't get him outside."

By then we'd reached the library. I looked over at Bill, who seemed engrossed by the books. "Bill," Mint said, "would you like to come outside now?

All the other guests are outside, waiting for Ruprecht to make a speech."

"A speech?" Ruprecht said in horror, his eyebrows shooting up. He hesitated for a moment. "Oh, yes, I'd like you to hear my speech, Bill."

Bill chuckled. "No offence, Ruprecht, but I don't want to hear your speech. Perhaps someone will sum it up for me later." He chuckled to himself at his own joke.

Suddenly, Bill turned away from the endless supply of books with a look of dread on his face. "What was that? Did you feel that tremor?"

Mint gasped, staring directly at him. "Oh no, did you all feel it too?"

Ruprecht and I nodded, but I had not felt a thing, and I was sure that Bill was the only one who had.

"We all need to get outside where it's safe," Ruprecht said.

"There are no earthquakes in this area, though," Bill said, rubbing his chin.

"That's what they said in Newcastle in 1989," I said. "They'd never had a quake there before, until that big one hit."

Bills face went white, and he clung to the

nearest bookshelf. "There's another one! Let's get out of here!"

"Yes, let's go," Mint said, heading for the door.

To my relief, Bill followed her, but just as she reached the door, it violently slammed shut in front of us.

Mint and Ruprecht both tried the lock but it wouldn't open.

"The tremors have jammed the door!" Bill said, with fear in his voice

I hadn't felt a single tremor, and I knew the house was doing it to Bill. However, the door would not open, and I wondered what would happen if we couldn't get Bill outside.

"What the…?" Bill said.

I looked behind me. Books flew from their shelves. At first, it all happened slowly, one or two books at a time. I watched in horror as the pace picked up and the tomes were tossed to and fro. I tugged on the doorknob, but it wouldn't budge. Regardless of what I tried, the door seemed to be cemented shut.

Ruprecht took a turn. "I think the locking mechanism broke." He continued to fidget with the lock.

All of a sudden, Bill screamed. "Oh my gosh!" he yelled, stumbling back towards the doorway. Both his hands were up, like a lion tamer hoping to keep the books at bay.

I turned back to him thinking he was afraid of the flying books, but it was apparently now the walls. Bill was ducking, shielding his face with one hand, and his other hand was pressed against the wall.

There was a muted, screeching noise that sounded as if the bookcases and the walls behind were closing in on their target. It all looked perfectly normal to me, but it was just as obvious to me that Bill was seeing a very different scene. After just a few seconds, the noise was much louder and much more menacing. It sounded like an evil creature scraping its claws against the walls as it was pushing them in.

Despite his fear, Bill must have noticed that the three of us were not afraid. "Can't you see it?" he yelled.

"See what?" I said.

Ruprecht walked over to the distressed man, and gently laid his hands on his shoulders. "Bill, I need you to listen to me. Perhaps you've had too much to drink. That was what my speech was going to be about. We served strong wine before we served the food. If you've had too much wine on an empty stomach, you must be seeing things. Do you feel dizzy?"

Bill Gafney slowly looked up, and his face looked less stricken. "Yes, I feel so dizzy! Yes, I did drink. Why?" he asked, his breathing laboured.

"Like I said, some of the wine has proven to be stronger than usual," Ruprecht said, his tone even. "Are you hallucinating? Are you seeing things that aren't really happening but feel real to you?"

I watched on, admiring Ruprecht's calm manner. The man nodded and smiled, like an immense weight had suddenly been lifted from his shoulders. He took one step, then fell to the floor again, his hands firmly over his eyes. "I can't! I can't!" he wailed. "I think I'm going to be sick."

Ruprecht patted Bill on the shoulder. "Listen, if you're seeing things that aren't there, just stand in the centre of the room and close your eyes. Breathe carefully and by the time you open them again, we'll be on our way to get some air, okay?"

Bill nodded repeatedly, closing his eyes as he stepped into the middle of the room. "Just please hurry and get that door unlocked."

"I will," Ruprecht said firmly. "Keep your eyes

firmly shut, and let me lead you out of the house. Let's get you outside for some fresh air. You'll feel much better outside," he said, helping Bill to his feet.

I continued to fidget with the doorknob. As the sounds grew louder, I looked over my shoulder to see that the books were dropping off the shelves again.

"Stop it!" I yelled at the house.

At that moment the door opened, much to my shock.

I felt something tickling my legs. I glanced down to see that Hawthorn and Willow were now wrapped around my ankles. "What do you two want?" I said.

Bill ran past us all. He sprinted down the hallway and out the front door, which mercifully opened for him.

Ruprecht, Mint and I followed him outside. "What's wrong with him?" a lady I'd never met asked Ruprecht.

"He just remembered that he'd left the iron on," Mint said, as Bill disappeared down the street on foot.

I looked back at Ruprecht. "Him, too? Three of them? How is that possible?"

Ruprecht raised his eyebrows. "That makes no sense at all," he said, scratching his head. "Something must be wrong. Surely the three of them weren't in it together. We all need to talk."

I nodded at Ruprecht, and when I turned away, I found that Mint had disappeared. I figured that Camino and Thyme had gotten Dermott Smith and Jason Mackay home safely, since I hadn't heard any other screams. I hurried down the hallway towards the library, and when I got there, everything seemed normal.

Mint was in the library, putting books back on the shelves. "So, what happened?" she asked, looking at Ruprecht.

He shook his head, clearly baffled. "I'm not quite sure. It appears that Amelia's home doesn't like any of the three suspects."

"So which of them is the killer?" Camino asked.

Ruprecht sighed. "I don't know which of them committed the act. Actually, I don't know *if* any of them did it, either."

"Oh boy," Thyme added. She groaned as she slouched down deep into the loveseat, rubbing her head. "I was Dermott Smith's captive audience while I was trying to do damage control. I guess this party was a bad idea after all."

I slumped down on my couch with a groan. Even my eyelashes and toenails felt exhausted. I found parties arduous in general, but this one had really taken the cake. I could swear that I could hear the house grumbling crankily. Ruprecht and the other ladies looked drained as well. "Sorry." I shot Thyme a sympathetic smile. It had taken forever to round up the three troublemakers. I'd say it was like rounding up a herd of cats, except cats were more cooperative.

"This might not have been the best idea," Mint said.

"You think?" Thyme said irritably, and then gave us an apologetic smile for the tone in her voice.

"So in the end, the house saw all three as dangerous, or at least unsavoury, enough to expel." Ruprecht sighed and rubbed at the bridge of his nose. "I'm afraid we caused you a great deal of trouble for naught, my dear."

"Not at all." I shook my head. "I did get to meet a few people tonight. And I guess it's good to know that the house comes with its own security system, but what do we do now? The house didn't narrow down the list at all."

"It can't be helped," Ruprecht said in a kindly voice. "We will just need to keep an eye on them the old fashioned way. Hopefully, someone will show their true colours."

CHAPTER 18

I stepped through the front door of the cake store, holding a large white sign with red writing on it. Thyme was behind the counter, cleaning the top of it with a dust rag. Ruprecht and his granddaughter, Mint, were there as well, each of them standing near the counter, eating a cupcake.

"Have you guys seen this?" I asked excitedly, flipping the sign around and holding it in front of my chest so the others could read it.

"Yeah," Thyme said, glancing over. "They're all over town. Popped up a couple of months ago."

"Do you know why?" I asked. I thought I might have found a motive for Brant McCallum's murder. The sign was only one of many, and they were posted all around town. They all read the same

175

thing, 'No Coal Seam Gas,' all in the same blocky crimson lettering.

"Some people are worried drilling for the gas could upset things around here. So what?" Mint asked.

"Well, do you know who owns the property the gas was found on first?" I asked. "Well, I should say 'owned.'"

"Yes, it was Brant. I remember him making a big fuss about it," Thyme said.

"That's when the signs went up," Mint added. "Almost everyone here was against drilling for it. Brant seemed as though he was going to do it anyway."

I sighed and tossed the sign onto the counter. "I thought I had come across a motive, but you guys already know all about it. How come nobody said anything about it? I mean, if Brant was going to drill for coal seam gas, well, surely that seems like a motive for someone, right?"

"I don't know," Ruprecht said, speaking up now that he had swallowed the last bit of his cupcake. "It was a flash in the pan. He wanted to drill, but everyone was against that, and I guess it turned out that he couldn't drill anyway. He had some people come in, guys in big trucks with hard hats, real official type stuff. They said he didn't have enough on his land to warrant drilling."

"I just googled it on my phone," I said. "He owned a lot of land. One hundred acres."

"It was at the edge of his land, I think," Ruprecht went on. "The signs just stayed up because no one felt like bringing them down, I guess."

I was deflated. "I thought I was onto something," I said, my head down.

"Hey, we have three good suspects, don't we?" Thyme said. "One of them is surely the culprit. Let's just stick to our plan, and do some recon after we close for the day."

I almost teased her for saying a word like 'recon.' "Actually," I said, "I found out more."

"What is it?" Thyme asked.

"Guess who owns the land right next to Brant's?"

Everyone shrugged.

"Melanie Simpson," I said, nodding as their jaws dropped. "Right next to his land, five hundred acres of it. It's likely the bulk of the gas is on her land."

"His fiancée?" Ruprecht asked.

"Yep," I said.

"And how did you find out all of this?" Mint asked.

"Google, of course."

Thyme laughed. "You're turning into quite the detective."

"I know!" I was quite pleased with myself.

"You know, Melanie and Brant couldn't have been more different," Mint told me. I still had not met the woman who had been willing to marry Brant.

"That's true," Ruprecht said, picking up the thread of discussion. "No one was really quite sure how they met. It's not like we talked about it much, but it is a small town, and Brant was well known to everyone. Something of the town celebrity, what with his car lot, and having those tasteless commercials that seemed to be more of a parody than anything. He did well for himself, at least."

"So we thought maybe that was it," Mint said. "Melanie was after his money. She was so quiet though, and well, shy, I guess you could say. She's lived here for years, and I've maybe spoken to her five times, if that. It's hard to say that about anyone here. We all know each other, and everyone knows everyone's business. You just hear things. Well, hearing that Melanie and Brant were engaged, that was literally the first major thing I'd ever heard about her. I'm not even sure what she does for a living."

"Whatever it is, it must keep her well to do," Thyme suggested. "That's a lot of land she owns, next to Brant's land."

"Maybe she inherited it," I said, thinking of my own recent situation.

Everyone nodded.

"She seems very environmental, though," Thyme added. "Melanie, I mean. She always has her own reusable bags at the grocery down the street, that sort of thing, and she drives a hybrid car."

"That's true," Ruprecht said. "She likes to read, and comes into my shop to buy antiques. I guess I see her more than anyone in town, but she doesn't really speak. She's friendly enough, but doesn't go out of her way for small talk. Brant, on the other hand…"

Mint interrupted him. "I'm not even sure he could read, and he never shut up."

The others laughed, but it was a laugh that trailed off somewhat awkwardly. Brant had been a pain in the butt, and didn't have a lot of supporters in town, but still, the man was dead now, and the four of us standing in the cake store knew he had been murdered. Whatever kind of man he was when he was alive, his death at least deserved respect.

"So what do we do now?" I asked. "Is she on our list?"

"Our suspects list?" Thyme asked.

"Yeah," I said, looking from face to face.

"I think we should add her," Ruprecht said with a nod.

"I don't know," Mint said. "So she owns land next to him. That might even be how they met. But what would she want him dead for? Because of the land? The gas? She herself wouldn't want to drill, and there's a chance she has the land with all of the gas on it anyway. I don't know. I don't see the connection, really."

I looked at Thyme. She nodded. "Let's add her. I mean, it's always the spouse, isn't it? In the movies?"

The others laughed, but then Ruprecht spoke up. "This isn't a movie, though," he said in a solemn tone. "We need to be careful. This is real life, and someone murdered someone, and we might be on the trail of that killer. Who knows what's going on in their mind? Who knows what they could be capable of? We have to stay quiet, and do this right."

"So what's the next step, then?" I asked.

"Recon," Mint said with a smile, using Thyme's line. "But now we have another suspect."

"We could each take someone," Thyme suggested. "We could spend some time tailing each one, to see what they do."

"We shouldn't split up," Ruprecht said, shaking his head. "It could be too dangerous."

I thought for a moment. There were four of us, and we had four suspects who needed tailing. We could split into two groups of two. Aloud I said, "Yet what exactly were we supposed to catch someone doing? Sure, Brant was murdered, but did that mean his murderer would still be doing something illicit? Certainly not. It's probable that they won't be. They've achieved what they planned to do. Brant is dead. What else is there to do now? Whoever killed him has already done it. They're probably just living their normal life now."

Ruprecht rubbed his chin. "Yes, that makes sense. I suppose, if we're careful, we can each watch someone different. We can get started right away, and not have to worry about missing anything tonight."

No one argued with him.

"So how do we decide who takes whom?" I asked.

"You take Melanie," Ruprecht suggested. "You found her out, so it seems right."

I nodded. And then over the course of a quick five minutes, the others decided who they would follow. It was only half an hour until closing time, and I gave the go ahead to close up early. We had something to do, and we were all eager to get to it, if a little nervous.

CHAPTER 19

I turned onto the street where Melanie lived and quickly pulled over to the curb. The woman who would have married Brant lived on the edge of town, on a lonely street named Agrimony Lane. There were four houses here, two on the other side, spaced well apart before the street ended in a cul de sac. Melanie's house was the second on the left, situated just as the road bulged out into the turnaround.

The home was two stories tall, and grey. It was imposing looking, almost like something you would see in a horror film. The paint was peeling; the porch was wood and falling apart. There were no other cars parked on the street, apart from my car and another parked in the long driveway. I was worried that I stood out like a sore thumb, but there was nothing I could do.

I had planned to park and creep to the house on foot after I got there, but it was still light, and I was sure that could only end badly. But still, I had to do something. I thought that maybe I could walk around the block and head to the house from the back. That was better than nothing, so I turned off the engine and climbed quickly out of my car. As I was heading back to the street corner along the cracked and crumbling footpath, my phone buzzed in my jeans pocket. I pulled it out to see Thyme was calling me.

"I'm at Bill Gafney's place," she said in a hushed tone over the line. We still hadn't been able to find out what Brant McCallum had on Bill Gafney and his run to be elected, but it must have been big.

"Is he there?" I asked, as I walked and turned the corner onto Rue Street, the one that ran perpendicular to Agrimony Lane.

"No, but someone's watching TV in his living room. A woman. She has big hair, but I can't see much else, because the chair she's sitting in is pointing away from the window."

"Is it his wife?" I asked. Bill was married to a prim and proper woman named Charlotte, who was a few years his junior.

"No, I got word she's out of town. She teaches Bible study at the church, and she and a few others took the kids on a trip for a week."

"Girlfriend?" I asked.

"Maybe," Thyme said.

"Well, be careful," I cautioned her, lowering my voice to a whisper as I approached the house that sat behind Melanie's.

"You too," Thyme said, and the line went dead.

I crept through the side yard of a brown house which was both smaller than Melanie's and in better repair. The lawn was trim and there was a small flower bed running along the side of the house.

It wasn't dark yet, but it was heading that way. I left the brown house behind and cut across to the backyard of the large grey one. There were enough shadows to provide cover for me, but that didn't stop my heart from racing out of control. My palms were sweaty and I rubbed them on my sleeves.

A light was on in the grey house, on the ground floor. I peered through the window into the kitchen.

There was a refrigerator against the wall, and stone countertops alongside it. Melanie didn't appear to be in the kitchen, but I was too nervous to look straight in. I moved alongside the house and peered in through the window from the side. Now I could see more of the kitchen, including the stove. It was an older model gas stove, and it didn't look like it was used much. I wondered if Melanie was a vegan. I bet the woman ate a lot of salads. I couldn't see Brant eating a lot of salads. The marriage was probably doomed from the start, but was even more so if Melanie had killed her husband to be.

And then the woman herself appeared, coming in through a swinging door much like the one in the cake store that separated the kitchen from a dark hall. Melanie Simpson was tall and young, with long blonde hair. She was wearing running shorts with a baggy pink tee shirt. She looked as though she might be going running, but first she opened the fridge.

I was interested to see what the woman took from the fridge, but then I heard a voice and my blood ran cold. I turned to see a small child standing next to me.

"What are you doing?" the kid asked again.

"Uh," I said, not sure of what to say. The child

looked to be about seven. He was wearing a dirty shirt and shorts, with small gym shoes on his feet. He looked like he had spent a good and eventful day outside. I wondered if he lived in the brown house.

"Are you a bad guy?" he asked.

"What?"

"A burger," the boy said. "Isn't that what they're called?"

I was confused for a moment, but then it dawned on me. "Oh, a burglar. No, I'm not a burglar, or a bad guy."

I was worried Melanie would hear us and come to investigate, so I moved away from her house as quietly as I could, with the child following me.

"So what are you doing?" the boy asked once more.

"I'm playing hide and seek. I don't want to be found," I said in a flash of brilliance.

"Oh!" the boy said, nodding. "Can I play?"

"Sure, is that your house?" I asked, pointing across the two back yards to the brown house.

"Yes, my mother and I live there."

"Okay, go hide in your yard. I'll tell my friend someone new is playing when she finds me."

"Okay!" the boy said, and he turned and ran for the house.

I felt bad for disappointing the kid, but when I turned to look into the window again, the kitchen was empty. It was also now dark. I was thinking about moving around to the front when I heard a car start from that direction. "Shoot!" I said somewhat too loudly. I hurried around to the front of the house, just in time to see Melanie's blonde head in her car as it zoomed down the street. I watched the woman turn left.

"Shoot, shoot, shoot!" I said to no one in particular as I threw myself into my car and started the engine. I backed all the way out into the street, and hurried off in Melanie's direction.

Melanie's car was blue, and I was pretty sure I saw it up ahead, with two cars in between us. I fell into a relaxed pace as I followed her. Melanie turned this way and that, and soon there were no cars between us to keep me hidden, so I fell back a distance.

Melanie headed out of town for the countryside, and after fifteen minutes of driving pulled into a small gravel parking area at the foot of a couple of walking trails. She parked and got out, and hurried down one trail.

I considered what I could do, but I had to go for it. I parked as well and then got out, making a show of stretching my legs before I hurried down the same walking trail that Melanie had gone down.

I tried to stay back, but if the other woman were to turn around, there was nowhere for me to hide. Well, there were plenty of places to hide, but I figured it would be weird if I dived behind a tree. Luckily for me, Melanie didn't turn around. She kept her head down as she walked, and I could see the bluish glow of a mobile phone screen in front of her. Was she texting? Was she meeting someone out here in the bushland? Maybe for payment? Payment for a murder? My head spun as more and more possibilities filled it.

Suddenly Melanie stopped and bent down. I paused, moving off the trail and actually sliding behind a large old gum tree. I felt like an idiot, but it was the only plan I had. I peeked around the tree and saw Melanie digging in the dirt, next to the trail. I hadn't noticed the small trowel the woman had brought with her, but I could see it plainly now.

Melanie dug up a small box and opened it. She pulled something out of it and slid it into her pocket. Then she put something else in it, reburied the box, and turned towards me.

I ducked back behind the tree. I was pretty sure that Melanie hadn't seen me, and she walked back towards the parking lot. I let her go and then went to the spot where she had reburied the box. The earth there was soft and I could pull it up easily, and soon I had a small metal box held in one hand. I opened the lid with the other.

Inside the box was a small piece of paper. 'Too late,' it read, in slanting scrawl.

What did it mean? I had no idea. I was frustrated. Too late? Who was too late? It dawned on me that Melanie might have known she was being followed after all, and the note was meant for me. No, surely if the woman knew I was there, she would have said something.

I had nothing left to do but bury the box as fast as I could and hurry back to the parking lot. I did so, and once again arrived in time to see Melanie driving away. I had no way of knowing if she was going home, so I decided I needed to follow her once more.

Melanie's car turned onto the road in the opposite direction to town. As I waited to follow her at a safe distance, my phone rang. It was Thyme.

"It's him!" she yelled, before I could answer. "He's the woman!"

"What?" I asked, as I slowly pulled onto the road.

"Bill Gafney is the woman. He got up to get a snack. It's him, in a wig and a dress! He's wearing stockings and heels! It's him!"

I burst out laughing. "Poor guy. Well, we now know what Brant had on him," I said after I caught my breath.

"Yeah. It's a doozy. I'm going to keep watching him. You know, he looked better in that dress than I would have, seriously."

I laughed.

"How are things on your end?" Thyme asked.

"Strange. I'll fill you in tonight," I said, and then I ran out of mobile service. Melanie was pulling into another parking lot, at the head of another trail.

I followed her once more, and once more she dug up a box. I checked it out after she was gone, and this time there was a pencil inside. I couldn't figure out what any of it meant. This was getting weirder and weirder. Yet again I followed her at a distance. She walked down the trail with her mobile phone out, and she dug up another box. I decided to go for broke. As the woman was opening the box,

I walked up to her. I figured she didn't know who I was.

"Hi, what do you have there?" I asked, trying to be as nonchalant as I could.

"Oh, it's a couple things," the woman said, rising and turning. "You geocaching too?"

"Geocaching?"

"Yeah, I figured you got here like I did."

"No, I don't know what that is," I admitted. "I'm, um, out collecting eucalyptus leaves for my garden." I silently berated myself. What a stupid thing to say! I wasn't even holding a bag to collect my supposed leaves.

"Oh, yes, they make good mulch," Melanie said.

Who knew!

She kept speaking. "Someone buries something, and then they post the location, in coordinates, on a website. You have to use GPS to find it. The first one gets what's inside. This one has a couple bucks and some old buttons from the thirties. Pretty cool stuff."

"I've never heard of any of that in my life," I said.

Melanie laughed. "I got into it a little while ago. I love it. I…" she paused then, and even in the falling light, with the sun so well blocked by the tall trees around us, I could see the woman's eyes shining with tears. "I had a friend who did it with me. Well, he was more than a friend." She sniffled. "He died, and I just, well, I thought that he would always be with me, but he isn't."

I smiled and nodded. "He is," I said. "If you feel him, he's here." I hoped that was the right thing to say.

"He showed me about this. No one knew he did it, but he loved coming out and finding treasure. He said it made him feel like a kid again, playing pirates in the back yard. It's kind of like that, digging something up."

"It seems like fun," I said, trying to be comforting.

"I should get going," Melanie said. "Don't get lost out here."

"Yeah, I'm going to go a bit further and then head back," I said.

"Here," Melanie said, holding out a button. "Take this. Your first treasure."

I reached out and took the button slowly. "Thank you." It was made of tin and had a sharp spike on the back. It indeed looked like it was old.

Melanie nodded, and then turned around and

headed for the road. I watched her go, and then started walking after her. I had wasted so much of my day, following a woman I was now convinced hadn't done anything. As I drove home, I thought of the tears in the poor woman's eyes.

CHAPTER 20

*I*t wasn't quite closing time, but Thyme and I both thought that no one would be coming in at this hour. Besides, it was only cranky customers who came in right at closing time. At the moment, there weren't many customers, cranky or otherwise, what with all the rumours that cake from my store had killed Brant McCallum.

And this all led to my first lesson in witchcraft, in the store's back room. I kept throwing nervous glances over my shoulder, as if someone would sneak up on us and ask us what we were doing. But no one was there, and no one was coming, so I turned back around to face Thyme and concentrate on the task at hand.

Thyme was holding a wooden box, as big a shoe

box perhaps, with a hinged lid. She sat on the floor of the back room and motioned for me to do the same. I sat across from her, folding my legs beneath me. Thyme put the box in her lap and flipped open the lid. She pulled out a yellow candle first, thick and waxy looking, and set it on the floor. The next thing she extracted was a small plastic baggie with green herbs inside it. She set the box to the side and prepared the area between us.

The herbs were placed on the ground in a particular pattern, and then the candle was placed upon them, though the long stemmed herbs poked out from beneath the candle. "This can help us find out what killed Brant," Thyme said, and although I wasn't quite sure how some herbs and a candle were going to help, I thought it best not to say that, so I just nodded.

Before Thyme could go further with the spell, the front door to the cake store chimed as it was opened. I had been wrong. Someone had come in right before closing time.

"I'll get it," I said, standing quickly. I went through the swinging door out into the shop and froze. There were two police officers standing just inside the shop, the man and the woman who had come when Brant had died.

"Hello," Constable Stevens said as she pulled off her hat. The male cop left his on.

"Hi," I said, stopping at the counter. "Can I help you with anything?"

"As much as I'd love a cupcake, I better watch my diet," the woman cop said with her trademark wide, and I suspected, fake smile. The male cop, Sergeant Greer, seemed content to hang back and let his partner do the work, wherever the work was today.

Constable Stevens held something in her hand, a manila envelope like one would find in any number of office buildings across the world, and she opened it as she moved to the counter. She pulled a single sheet from the envelope and stared at it. "Mind if I ask you a few questions?" she said after a moment.

"No," I said. I was quite nervous.

"Do you guys use any old rat poison around here?" Reed asked.

I shook my head. "Is that what killed Brant McCallum? Rat poison? So you don't think it was natural causes anymore?"

The female cop smiled as Sergeant Greer busied himself back by the door, gazing out of the window there as if he were on a stake out, although I was reasonably sure he had an ear attuned to the conversation at the counter.

"I'm sorry. It's all strictly confidential. I'm sure you understand," she said.

"Sure," I said, and behind me the door to the back room swung open and Thyme came out.

"What's going on?" she said.

"Just a few questions," Constable Stevens said again. "I was asking Ms Spelled if you ever used rat poison here, particularly any older brands. Maybe you would know if you guys ever used it?"

"No, never," Thyme said, shaking her head. "We love animals here, even the so-called pests. We had a mouse problem a couple years ago, but we used traps that didn't harm the animals. We baited them with peanut butter and then let them go down by the creek."

Stevens nodded. "I see. Well, would you guys mind if we looked around?"

I knew that the cops couldn't look if I didn't allow them too, but I figured that would make them annoyed as well as suspicious, so I nodded. "Sure, go for it." I hoped Thyme had cleared anyway all evidence of the spell.

"Great," Stevens said with her irritating smile. She turned towards Sergeant Greer, who came striding forward. They didn't spend any time out on the shop itself, but they went straight to the back room. I was relieved beyond measure that Thyme had cleared up the candle and herbs. The box remained out, sitting on a nearby counter, and Stevens flicked it open with a fingertip and looked inside it, although she was apparently uninterested in the contents and closed it quickly.

"When did you say you had a problem with mice?" Stevens asked.

"A couple of years ago," Thyme said. "When we had that really rainy spring. The creek rose, and it sent the mice from the bushland all over town."

"I remember the rain," Stevens said, nodding. Her partner still hadn't spoken. The two cops moved around the back room without another word, peering in boxes, lifting them up. Finally, they seemed satisfied and they went back out into the show room.

"Thanks," Stevens said at the door with a smile that showed every tooth she had. The male cop had already headed out the door, and wasted no time climbing behind the wheel of the police vehicle parked at the curb in front of the cake shop. *Another good sign for potential customers*, I thought sarcastically.

By the time I locked the door behind them, we were officially ten minutes past closing time.

"So it was something that shows up in rat poison," Thyme said after the door was locked.

I nodded. "But *old* rat poison, right? That's the way she made it sound. Like it was something that wasn't in rat poisons made today."

Thyme tapped her chin. "Clever of you to catch that," she said. "Maybe whatever it was, was too dangerous. They took it off the market."

I shrugged. "Maybe."

"If we could find out what it could be, that could help us out with this spell. I have to set parameters, and if we had a smaller list, it would go faster."

"Well then, let's check it out," I said, leading the way to the back room. There was a small table in the room in the far corner, next to the rear door which led out to the alley that ran behind the shop, and contained a dumpster. On the table was an older model computer, but the internet was good, and I hadn't seen the need to update.

I sat in a metal folding chair and Thyme leant forward next to me, her hands palm down on the table.

"Where do we start?" I asked, already googling 'old rat poisons' before Thyme had a chance to answer. "Thyme?" I said, as she was staring off at the far wall.

"You know, I've just remembered something," she said. "Brant came to the shop once, not too long before your aunt died, and he was complaining that his hair was falling out. Doesn't arsenic cause hair to fall out? Probably other poisons do, too."

I shrugged and typed in, 'Poisons that cause hair loss.'

We spent a few minutes going through the search results, and Thyme took notes. After ten or so minutes, we had a list of poisons known to cause hair loss: arsenic, boric acid, thallium, meadow saffron, and lead. These could all lead to hair loss if introduced regularly to the body.

"Now we have to cross check to see if any of these things were in old rat poison," I said. My next search, 'old rat poison ingredients,' was a good guess, because in only a few minutes of searching a couple different pages we had the list narrowed down from five to three. Arsenic, thallium, and lead had all once been used in rat poison, but had all been banned in the last few decades.

Thyme scribbled out the poisons that hadn't made the cut. "Okay, that helps a lot," she said as the two of us sat back down on the floor, and she set up the spell once more.

She laid out the herbs. "Althea," she said, "for truth. Calamus root and liquorice root for compulsion."

She set down the candle and then lit it with a silver lighter. She then reached to her neck and pulled up a piece of clear quartz that hung from a gold chain. She tugged the chain over her head and held it up for me to see.

"You need to get yourself one of these, girl," Thyme said. "It's a pendulum. I use it a lot."

"What does it do?" I asked.

"I'll write the names of the three poisons and the pendulum will swing over the poison that killed Brant McCallum."

I clasped my hands together with delight. "Well, we can do that to find out his killer!" I exclaimed. "We can write the names of all the suspects on pieces of paper, and the pendulum can tell us who the murderer was."

Thyme shook her head. "It doesn't work like that. It would be great if it did. I know all the suspects."

"So?" I was puzzled.

"Thinking gets in the way," she said. "I know the suspects personally, so I'm attached to the outcome, even if subconsciously. If I have any information, the pendulum will be influenced."

I pulled a long face, trying to take it all in.

"I'll show you how it works." Thyme took up the notebook again. She wrote the three poisons on a separate sheet of paper for each and then tore them out. She placed them at the three equal points around the candle. She then took the quartz and held it by the end of the chain. She let it dangle over the flame of the candle. Slowly, it began to rock.

I thought Thyme must have been moving it on purpose, but as I watched her hand, I realised she wasn't moving at all. Her fingers were as still as a statue. The crystal was moving on its own. The rocking became more like a circle, growing wider.

Suddenly, the quartz swung in the direction of one piece of paper, and then hovered over it. I leant forward to read the page. Written in Thyme's loopy, large scrawl was one word, 'thallium.'

"There you go," Thyme said, smiling as she flicked her wrist and the chain fell. She stood up, picked up a silver candle snuffer, and then used it to extinguish the flame. Smoke, grey and thick, curled up from the wick. Thyme took the candle and put it back in the box, and then gathered up the herbs.

"So now we know what killed Brant," I said.

CHAPTER 21

I stood in the back room, staring with horror at the cupcakes. Thyme was busy out front in the show room. I thought that was a silly name for the front of the cake store. It made me think of car sales, but Thyme was used to calling it that. I didn't think I could get her to change now. Even if I could, I didn't have an alternate name for it.

Thyme had left me alone in the kitchen to take a batch of cupcakes out of the oven, and to put the icing on an already cooked batch of cupcakes.

I hurried to the oven when the timer sounded. I tugged on two oven mitts and reached in with both hands, pulling out a hot pan of cupcakes. I left them on top of the oven to cool. I slipped off the oven mitts and turned my attention to the cooling rack laden with cakes on the counter.

Thyme had set everything out that I would need, in a few different stations. There was a mixing station and a decorating station, with everything ready to go in the order it would be needed.

The cooling rack held red velvet cupcakes, and I regarded them with fear. It was time for the icing. Despite the fact that Thyme and Ruprecht had told me over and over again that my problem was simply with fire, and that in turn meant that I would be a talented kitchen witch once I could control the fire, the thought of anything to do with baking filled me with trepidation, if not outright horror.

With Thyme's words that colouring icing was one of the easiest tasks in the kitchen ringing in my ears, I got right to it. Thyme had earlier demonstrated a very neat looking red and white swirl icing, so I would need to colour some of the icing red. She had put a line of the red icing and a line of plain white icing in a pastry bag. When she squeezed the tip and piped the icing high on the cupcake, it came out in a swirl.

I put some of the white icing into a smaller bowl and set it on the counter. There was a line of food colouring up on the small shelf above the counter, and I reached for the red. As I did, my hand brushed a smaller bottle. It tipped over and the small rubber cork fell out and into the icing bowl. Before I could react, the contents of the bottle had emptied into the icing.

"Shoot," I said. The material from the bottle smelled strongly of strawberries, and I figured that was exactly what it was. Red strawberry flavouring. There simply wasn't enough icing made to start over, and judging by the muffled voices I heard out on the show floor, there wasn't enough time to make a whole new batch. I used a spatula to get the cork out of the icing.

A few minutes later, the icing was mixed and in the pastry bag. I took some time to pipe the icing onto the red velvet cupcakes, and then I took the tray and hurried out to the counter. Thyme was busy serving. She was used to this, and she was in her element. I knew Thyme would be happier if she could make everything in the back forever, but she also knew that I had to start somewhere. That is why she had put me where I would do the least damage. Or so she thought.

I was mixing the icing for the double chocolate chip cupcakes when I heard Thyme calling my name. I thought I detected a note of panic in her voice, so I stopped what I was doing and rushed out into the show room.

There were two customers. I recognised the first, a regular customer. She was in her fifties, had a sharp face with a nose like a hawk's beak, and was the principal at the local Catholic school. She was very proper, and rather uptight. That's why I found it quite odd that the woman had taken off one of her thick tan stockings and was now twirling it over her head.

As I watched, the woman let the stocking sail towards the other person in the shop. This was also a regular customer, Mr Reynolds, a man of around sixty with a huge nose that was so red it looked like a tomato. His eyes were beady and small, and his teeth yellow and crooked. He had never been married, and likely never would be. His attitude was even worse than his looks.

The stocking landed on his shoulder, and he picked it off with a look of disgust. "I don't know what's gotten into you, lady, but you need to stop," he said.

"I'll stop when you love me!" the woman shouted.

"Mrs Clutterbuck, are you all right?" Thyme asked.

"I'm perfect," the woman answered in a shrill voice. "My prayers have been answered! I've never seen a man more perfect for me!"

"If this is some kind of joke, it needs to stop!" Mr Reynolds said.

I turned to Thyme. "What's happening?"

"You're watching it!" Thyme said. "She ordered a cupcake, had one bite, and then she hugged Mr Reynolds. Then she took off her stocking and threw it at him."

"Yes, I saw that part," I said. "I couldn't miss it."

"Tell me you love me!" she wailed.

Mr Reynolds backed away. "I don't even know your name!"

"And I don't know yours!" Mrs Clutterbuck said. "Mine is Claudia. Do you like it? Oh, learning about someone, the first part of new love, I adore it. I adore you! Please, tell me your name! Tell me everything about you. I have to know!" She flung herself forward, and slid her arms around him.

He shot me a pleading look. "I only wanted a cupcake! What kind of place are you running here?" he asked.

Thyme took me by the arm. "Did you put anything in these cupcakes?" she whispered. "She had a red velvet cupcake."

I blanched. "I dropped some strawberry flavouring into it."

"Oh no!" Thyme shook her head.

"It wasn't strawberry flavouring, was it?" I asked.

"I don't think so. A little brown bottle with a black rubber stopper?"

"Yes."

"It was a love potion," Thyme said.

I looked over at Mr Reynolds. He had his arm up to protect his face as Claudia Clutterbuck tried to press her lips to his.

"I'll have to whip up an antidote. She bit into it, and fell in love with the first man she saw. It takes months to wear off, so I have to reverse it. I'm sorry. I didn't clean up like I should have. That should have never been out."

I wasn't sure why Thyme even had a love potion, and then for an amusing minute I thought about what I could do with a vial of the stuff, but as Thyme went through the swinging door to the back, Mr Reynolds brought me out of my thoughts and back to the situation.

"I would like to leave!" he said firmly to Mrs Clutterbuck, who was blocking the exit.

"Take me with you. Tell me your name!" Claudia Clutterbuck said, before she peppered his cheek with kisses.

"It's Franklin!" the man screamed as he finally pushed her away. She was already going back for him when I ran around the counter and put my hands on her arms.

"Quick, go!" I yelled, and Mr Reynolds nodded and hurried for the door.

"No! My love! Franklin! What wonderful times we'll have!" Mrs Clutterbuck screamed, but when the object of her desire disappeared out the door, she burst into tears and practically fell down. The only thing keeping her from crumpling to the floor was my arm. "You sent him away! My love! We were to be married!"

"I don't think he proposed, exactly," I said.

The older woman sighed sharply. "Well, we were to be engaged at some later date. I just know it!"

I nodded and patted the woman's head as she cried more. "Well, you know, they say true love can conquer anything," she said. "So a little time apart, that'll be nothing." She appeared to perk up. She got to her feet, but I kept a hand on her, in case she tried to tear out of the door after the man she suddenly loved. "I love him more than anything. Have you ever loved anyone?"

I thought it best to humour her. "I thought I did."

"Who was your first? Franklin wasn't my first love, but he was my greatest, so I guess we broke that mould."

"The first boy I had a crush on was named Ean Jackson," I said. "We went to high school together."

"Ah," Claudia sighed as she clasped her hands together, as if she were praying. "Young love!"

"Not exactly. He didn't feel the same about me."

"You should have told him how you felt!" the older woman said. "Think of what your life could have been. You never know. One little question, and things end up different."

"Yes, you're right," I said. Five minutes ago I hadn't even known that a love potion was real. It was just another thing in the long list of witch-related facts I had no trouble accepting these days. Thyme had said 'love potion,' and I had gone right along with it. It was strange.

Thyme came through the swinging door and

held up a small vial. She motioned me over. "She needs to drink this," she said. "Where's the guy?"

"He ran as soon as he could."

"I would've, too."

I grinned and took the vial. I turned to Mrs Clutterbuck. "You should have a drink of this," I said.

"No, I couldn't!" She shook her head. "I don't feel thirsty. I feel nothing but the fiery love I have for Franklin. Oh, my Franklin, when will I see his face again?"

"Franklin told me he loves women to drink this," I said, saying the first thing that came into my head.

"Really?" Mrs Clutterbuck's brow quirked. She stepped forward and snatched up the vial. She tilted her head back and swallowed the contents in one gulp.

The change was immediate. The woman seemed to calm, seemed to become herself as soon as the liquid was down her throat. She shook her head softly. "What's going on?" she asked. "Where am I?"

"The cake store," I said, "Are you okay?"

"Yes, I just feel odd. What happened? Why do I feel like this?"

"It's a long story," I said.

"You had a bit of a spell," Thyme said, as she smirked at me. "You should be okay now. Would you like some water?"

"Yes, please. My throat is a bit dry, and my heart is beating so fast. It feels strange."

"It's all over now," I said, going to the counter and taking the cup of water from Thyme. I handed it to Mrs Clutterbuck and watched her down it.

"I just have one more question," Claudia Clutterbuck said.

Thyme and I looked at each another. I wasn't sure what the woman was going to say. I wasn't sure if she remembered anything. She seemed not to, but I steeled myself for the question anyway.

"Yes?" I asked, tentatively.

"Why is my right leg colder than the left?"

CHAPTER 22

I sighed as I stood behind the counter of the cake shop. I was staring at the door. It hadn't been opened in hours. In fact, the last person who had opened it was Thyme, when she arrived at work in the morning.

"People still think we killed Brant. I'm sure they think we did it accidentally, but still…" Thyme came through the swinging door to stand next to me at the counter.

I shook my head. "We'll figure it out. We just need to figure out how to get the people back into this place."

Thyme nodded. "We just need to prove it wasn't us."

"You're right," I said. "And we're trying, but all we've found out so far is that one politician likes to wear dresses, and that Melanie digs up secret boxes."

Thyme laughed. "So what's our next step?"

I wasn't sure how to answer that. I didn't know what we could do now. We had followed all four of our suspects, and been unable to find out anything about them that would indicate they had murdered Brant. For the most part, they all seemed relatively normal.

In fact, both of us had began to wonder if we were on the wrong track altogether. Maybe there was someone we had missed, a suspect we weren't even considering. A man like Brant had made a lot of people mad, so surely there was someone else out there. Thyme and I had discussed that fact the previous day.

"What if it wasn't meant for Brant?"

I didn't understand. I turned and looked at her. "What do you mean?"

"Just, what if Brant got poisoned, but he wasn't supposed to?"

"You think it was some crazed person trying to kill at random? But if that's the case, I don't know how we could ever prove it, so I think we should just focus on our four. Plus if it was a homicidal maniac, they surely would've killed again."

Thyme bit her fingernail. "I suppose you're right. Well, what do you want to do now? We can call Ruprecht and Mint, do some more recon."

I laughed. "You and that 'recon' word," I said. "No, I think we can stick together today, me and you."

"What do you have in mind?"

"You ever heard of dumpster diving?"

Thyme laughed and nodded. "I have, and I don't think I'm going to enjoy today."

Ten minutes later the two of us were locking the shop, having made the decision to close early so we could visit our four suspects' homes during the day, while they were all likely to be at work. We were going to go through their garbage, and we had decided it would be much easier not to be discovered in that act. We knew that we wouldn't find any evidence of rat poison, but we thought we might turn up something. It was worth a try. Nothing else had worked so far.

We went to Bill Gafney's house first. The cross-dressing politician had been blackmailed by Brant after Brant somehow found out that Bill liked to wear women's clothing as often as he could, and had threatened to tell his wife. I felt sorry for Bill. After all, *I Am Cait* was one of my fave TV shows.

We parked on the street, near the rather large house. Neither of us got out right away.

"This isn't exactly legal, is it?" Thyme asked.

"I don't think so," I said. "But we have to do it."

"You're right. I just don't think jail would suit me."

"Well then, let's be fast," I said with a chuckle. I pushed open my door and climbed out of the car. Thyme and I walked briskly up the footpath, side by side. We then hurried up the sloping driveway to the closed garage, and went to the left, sliding around the side of the garage. There were the garbage cans, two large black plastic bins.

"Should we make sure no one is here?" Thyme asked, and I considered it.

"No," I said finally. "Let's just get this done."

And with that, we went to work. I was hoping perhaps we would come across a letter, maybe written by Brant, threatening Bill and demanding payment.

Only one bin had any garbage in it, and the other two sat empty. There were two plastic bags in the full bin, so I pulled them both out and handed one to Thyme. We set them on the ground and pulled the ties apart, and got to work. It was messy and unpleasant, but we got through it. When we were finished, we had absolutely nothing to go on.

"That's okay," I said, trying to look on the bright side. "One down, three to go."

We hurried back to the car and drove to the next suspect's house. Jason Mackay was the delivery man who had been sold a faulty van by Brant, and had gone on to lose his business. I felt something of a kinship with the man in a way. I too was in danger of losing my business because of the blustery car salesperson.

Jason's house was smaller, and his garbage more untidy and more unpleasant. Thankfully there was less of it, but once again we turned up nothing.

"Perhaps we're on the wrong track," Thyme said as she climbed into my car.

"We're only halfway through. Let's finish before we decide that," I said.

Dermott Smith had the nicest house of the three, even bigger than the politician's. It appeared that even though Brant had cost him a lot of money in a poker game, he still had plenty to fall back on.

Thyme and I sneaked around the side of his house and didn't see any garbage cans.

"Maybe he keeps them in the garage," I

suggested as we made our way back to the front of the house.

"Then we're out of luck," Thyme said as we stopped in front of the garage. It had room for two cars, and was attached to the house. As we looked helplessly at the large cream coloured door, there was a rumble, and the door began to move up.

"Move!" I whispered, pushing Thyme to the side. We hid around the corner of the house, and as we peered around the edge, I heard a car engine roar to life. A sports car edged into view. The driver gunned it, and the car shot off down the winding driveway. The door rumbled again, and started to close.

I didn't have time to think. I hurried around the corner of the home and sprinted for the door. I threw myself forward, under the door. I must have triggered an invisible beam, as the door went back up.

Thyme ran to the garage. "You are crazy, girl!" she said in a loud whisper.

I lay on the smooth concrete floor of the garage, on my back, panting. "I really want the customers to come back," I said.

Thyme reached down and helped me to my

feet, and then hurried over to press the button to shut the door.

The garage was well maintained, and there was barely anything inside it. Off to the side were two black garbage bins. Once again, we pulled the garbage out with our hands and went through it. It took us longer than the other two homes, but once again we found absolutely nothing that would indicate that the guy was a murderer. I sighed. "Let's look on the shelves for thallium," I said.

Thyme shook her head. "The cops would've searched, surely. And he'd have to be crazy to leave evidence like that lying around. We should get out of here in case he comes back."

I ignored her, and did a quick skim of the shelves. There were plastic boxes of nuts and bolts, a few wrenches, and some old cans of paint. All were neatly stacked. "You're right," I said. "This guy's a clean freak."

"Let's go." Thyme pulled me over to the door. She hit the button again, and it opened. To my relief, no one was outside. "You go out, and then I'll close it and duck under," she said.

"And now we're three down," Thyme said once we were back in the car.

"Let's keep going to Melanie's house," I said.

Melanie's garbage bins were sitting on the side of the road, their lids open.

"Collection day was two days ago," Thyme said. "She clearly hasn't bothered to take them in yet."

"Shoot," I said. I felt defeated. I wanted to cry, to scream. I didn't know what else to do. This had been the last idea, our last hope at catching someone with something, anything at all. We just needed clues, and that was exactly what we weren't getting. Without even bothering to get out of the car, I turned around in the cul-de-sac and headed for the cake store.

"Wait a minute," Thyme said. "We didn't check one place."

"What do you mean?" I asked.

"What about all that land she owns? Does Melanie have a home out there?"

"I'm not sure," I said, "but we should go check."

Instead of turning left towards the centre of town at the intersection, I turned right, and headed just out of town, where Melanie had five-hundred sprawling acres.

I wasn't quite sure where the land was, but with Thyme checking her mobile phone we eventually made it. The first thing I saw was a dirt road leading off the main road. It was surrounded by trees, so I couldn't see too far down the road as it curved and continued on through the trees. There was a mailbox there, but it was broken, just a piece of wood painted white jutting out of the ground, with the actual box part hanging loosely, its front facing directly towards the ground.

I pulled onto the dirt road. "Let's go see what we can find," I said. "Keep an eye out for any cars. We don't want her to catch us."

CHAPTER 23

The dirt road was bumpy, and the recent rain had made it even worse. Large ditches, carved out of the hard packed surface by water, crisscrossed here and there.

"I don't think your car was made for off-roading," Thyme said, gripping the hand support near the passenger window on the ceiling.

"Me, either," I said. I grimaced as we bounced upwards over a severe bump. As the dirt path turned this way, the trees began to thin until they were suddenly gone altogether. I could see a wide open paddock in front of us, with long grass and little blue wildflowers.

"Wow," Thyme said.

I agreed. "It's beautiful here."

There were two structures standing in the clearing, a semi-standing burned down house, and further on, a dilapidated wooden barn that was lurching precariously to one side.

"What happened here?" I asked Thyme.

"Nothing," she said. "This is typical of old farms in the country. They just let the old farmhouses and barns fall down. You see it everywhere."

"I didn't know that," I said. I pulled the car to a stop between the barn and the burned-out husk. The barn was bare timber, and the rusted iron roof was missing in places. One door was shut and the other one was wedged open. It must have been open for some time, as a young gum tree was growing through the middle of it.

The barn was dark in some places, but a shaft of light fell through a hole in the ceiling, providing enough light. It was full of stuff, including a faded green tractor that looked like it hadn't been used in thirty years. To the right were pens of sorts, divided by low wooden walls. I could imagine that pigs had been kept in there. At the back of the barn was a ladder leading up to the roost. I could see the remains of some old mouldy hay up there.

"I'm going to look up there," I said, pointing to the ladder.

"I'll check these boxes," Thyme said. "Be careful, though. The wood up on that level is probably rotten, and I don't know if that ladder's safe."

I pulled a face. "I'll see if the ladder's going to hold my weight, and if it will, I'll only climb to the top and have a look." The ladder was old. I tested my weight on the bottom two rungs and they looked sturdy enough. I gingerly climbed up it, worried my foot would go right through a rung.

When I reached the top, I gripped the edge of the timber boards that made up the upper level. There were a few bales of rotten hay, their edges white with mould. There were also gaps in the floorboards, so there was no way I could go to that side of the platform. However, there was an old shelf in front of me. It held some old jugs and some old bottles, along with one big bottle labelled 'Lucijet.' I'd come across that one in my googling of discontinued poisons. It was a deadly poison formerly used for dipping sheep to rid them of lice, back in the day. I figured that a farmer of decades ago had kept the poisons up here to keep them away from kids. I only hoped he hadn't kept the ladder up there then.

I moved forward to look at the poisons, and pushed the Lucijet aside. I was debating whether to inch forward further, when a bottle caught my eye.

It was a six-sided bottle and it had fallen down behind the container of Lucijet. I learned forward as far as I could, and my fingers closed around the bottle. I pulled it out to take a closer look.

My heart missed a beat. The top of the label said 'Poison.' Across the middle was a black banner, and on it in white reverse writing was the word 'Thall-rat.'

"Thyme, come here!" I called out.

"What is it?"

"Listen to this," I said. I read aloud. "The original thallium sulphate rat poison that kills quickly. Rats cannot detect Thall-rat because it is tasteless and odourless."

"Hand it down to me," Thyme said. "Be careful."

I handed it down to her and then carefully climbed the ladder.

Thyme shook the bottle, and I could hear liquid sloshing within it. "Is Melanie the murderer?" I asked her.

Thyme shrugged.

"But why would she just leave this stuff here, on her land?" I asked. "The cops could've easily found it."

"But they didn't," Thyme pointed out. "Obviously they don't suspect her. Obviously they haven't searched here. And here's another thing. What if she really doesn't have anything to do with this building? I mean, I know she owns the land, but it doesn't look like anyone's been in here in years. This is a really old bottle. People really used to use this stuff."

"True, and there were various poisons and herbicides up there in the loft," I said. "It could have nothing to do with her."

"Do you believe that?" Thyme asked.

"I don't know," I said. "There seriously were a lot of poisons up there."

Thyme looked worried. "I suppose we shouldn't have touched that bottle."

I hit myself on the forehead. "I'll put it back. I'll wipe our fingerprints off it first."

"If the cops do a search, they won't find Melanie's fingerprints on it," Thyme said.

I pulled a face. "Good point. She'd be stupid to leave her own fingerprints on it, though."

I climbed back up the ladder, wiped the bottle clean, and put it where I'd found it. "Why would she kill him?" I asked Thyme as soon as I got back down the ladder. "We still haven't figured out that part."

"What if we were thinking about it all wrong?" Thyme said. "We know she would never drill for that gas. Maybe Brant was going to marry her, so he would legally be able to drill here. Remember, he didn't have enough on his land."

I nodded. "That makes sense."

"He's a charming guy when he wants to be, so they say," Thyme continued. "At any rate, he was a good salesman. So he sells himself, makes her fall in love, but then somehow she finds out he wants her land, specifically to drill for the gas?"

"So she knows she has the thallium in her old barn and decides to kill him?"

Thyme shrugged her shoulders. "I don't know. But it's all starting to fit, don't you think?"

I had to nod. "It really is," I said. "And if the thallium's just left here, along with a lot of other old poisons, she can pretend she had nothing to do with it. It would even help maybe to look like someone was framing her."

"It'd be a good story for the police at least," Thyme said.

"But is Brant wanting to drill on her land enough of a reason to kill him?" I asked. "Some of these other people's lives were ruined by Brant."

"I think it's enough of a reason for Melanie,"

Thyme said. "She's an environmentalist. She's well known around town for it. She takes all of that stuff very seriously. She would be so adamant against drilling."

"Why not just call off the engagement?"

Thyme held up her hands. "I don't have a clue. So what do we do now? Do we go to the police?"

"I don't think we can," I said. "Can we? 'Oh hey, we've been breaking into people's places, and we found this!' They would lock us up."

Thyme nodded. "You're right."

"And it's still not enough to go on, but it's a good start."

"All right," Thyme said. "Let's keep looking in here."

"I might go and look in the house," I said.

Thyme shook her head. "Be careful in that place, will you? It might fall on you."

"I will," I said with a smile.

The house was an empty shell. It looked as if it had burned down many years ago. As I turned to go back to the barn, I had the unmistakable feeling that someone was watching me. The hair on the back of my neck stood up.

I walked forward a bit, and spun in a slow circle, my eyes on the trees at the edge of the clearing. I didn't see anyone. And then I thought I saw movement, over near the dirt path that led to the road. Maybe there was a flash of blue, someone's shirt. I couldn't be sure. I couldn't even be sure I had seen someone. Perhaps it was a kangaroo, but they are not blue. Yet I distinctly had that strange feeling, and thought I saw something.

As I watched, I thought I heard a car start in the distance. I stayed quiet, straining my ears, hoping to confirm what I thought I was hearing, but I couldn't. I had no way of knowing if I had really heard an engine. I felt uneasy.

"That was fast," Thyme said, as soon as I stepped into the barn.

I considered telling her what I had felt and what I had thought I heard, but I decided there was no point freaking her out. It was probably my imagination, after all.

"Nothing there," I said. "All destroyed. It was just an empty shell."

Thyme nodded and stood up straight. She had been kneeling in front of the boxes. "Just a lot of junk," she said. "Old rusted tools in one box, old rabbit traps in another."

I nodded. "Want to get out of here? We did good."

"Now we just have to figure out our next step," Thyme said.

"I'm starting to think that's all detective work is," I said with a smile. "Finding something really small, and then spending days figuring out what to do with it."

Thyme laughed. "If that makes you a good detective, then we're great ones."

As we drove back to the road, I looked for any evidence that another car had been there. I saw nothing, but then again, what would I see? It hadn't been raining, so there was no way I would see tire tracks on the hard ground. Once back on the road, I turned in the direction of town. I didn't see another car until we reached the edge of town. I kept glancing in the rear view mirror as I drove, expecting to see someone following me, but no one was.

Had I seen someone? I was still on edge. I felt as though someone had been watching me. I thought I had seen someone in blue, cutting through the eucalyptus trees near the clearing.

CHAPTER 24

I couldn't sleep. I tossed and turned on the bed as I stared at the walls and ceiling. The day's events kept playing through my head on an infinite loop. That's what I got for going to bed so early.

"Any suggestions?" I asked the ceiling as I lay there. Oh gosh, I was rapidly becoming a crazy cat lady, having long conversations with my cats, and now I was even talking to my house.

I wasn't quite sure what I expected, anyway. A cup of tea to appear? Some sort of creak or rumble in response? I smiled at myself and shook my head. I had no idea how to begin processing this whole new twist on my world. Living houses, love potions, magic, a house with feelings?

I sighed and got out of bed. I pulled on my robe

as I made my way towards the kitchen. If I wasn't going to get any sleep, I could at least get some paperwork done. Even with the lack of business, there was always some sort of paperwork to catch up with, and Aunt Angelica had done it all by hand. I was trying to convert the hard files onto an online file, in the hope I could get the system into some sort of order before things got busy.

I wondered what I was going to do about Melanie and the Thall-rat. Or was this just a red herring? Was the real murderer Dermott Smith, Bill Gafney, or Jason Mackay? Who knows, maybe even one of those men had planted the Thall-rat in Melanie's barn to frame her.

Should I go to the police? And how would they react to me searching Melanie's barn? I wasn't quite sure how I was going to avoid trespassing charges.

I wondered why such an avid environmentalist would have poisons on her property to begin with. I had always assumed that environmentalists were big on protecting animals, even rats. It seemed strange to me that Melanie didn't get rid of the stuff, but then again, she had a whole collection of poisons there. Did she even know it was there? Perhaps not. It didn't seem right that an environmentalist would have a deadly poison collection.

I stared at the half completed file on my computer, trying to concentrate on my work, but I was unable to shake off an uneasy feeling. I rubbed the back of my neck.

Should I call someone? I picked up my phone and thumbed through my contact list. I did not have the slightest idea if Thyme stayed up late. I supposed she might. There was a reason this was called the 'witching hour,' right?

I finally decided against it. If I had been trying to sleep and someone called at this hour, I would have been irritated. It wouldn't be right to assume that Thyme was available to chat just to help me shake off the undercurrent of anxiety that was plaguing me. It wasn't her problem that I was having trouble settling down.

"I know you're there," I called up at the ceiling. "What's going on?"

"Perceptive," a cold voice stated.

I suppressed a scream. I whirled around to seek out the source of the voice.

"Don't move," a menacing yet familiar voice spat.

My heart pounded. I froze, my hands hovering in front of me. There was a woman standing in the doorway leading into the living room, and there was a pistol aimed in my direction. A chill coursed through my veins as I willed my eyes to come into focus.

"Melanie?" I stared at the dark-clad feature. What was Melanie doing in my house? What was she doing with a gun? She was part of all those anti-everything rallies. Why would she have a gun, of all things? "What are you…?"

"Shut up." The edge in Melanie's voice sent cold chills down my spine. "Just shut up and tell me what you know."

I flinched and heard a faint whimper in the back of my throat. What was she talking about? And what was with the crazy eyes? I was afraid to ask what she wanted. I was afraid not to respond. What should I do?

My mind refused to answer. All I could see was a woman pointing a gun at me, spitting out commands and vague demands. She looked like she might even be looking for an excuse to pull the trigger.

"Tell me now," Melanie snapped.

"What do you want?" I asked timidly. I couldn't get out of this situation if I didn't know what Melanie wanted. What could she possibly want from me?

"Tell me what you know." Melanie enunciated each word slowly, as if she were speaking to a simple mind. Her face contorted in disgust as she kept the weapon trained on me.

"Know?" I blinked at her.

"Don't play stupid. I saw you at the barn."

"You did?" I said, and flinched as the woman gave me a scathing sneer.

"Yes, you idiot," Melanie snapped. She looked nothing like the woman I had been keeping an eye on. Her hand wasn't wavering on that trigger, despite how long she had been holding it. She looked like she was very comfortable with a weapon, and she looked way too comfortable pointing it at me.

The woman gave a long suffering sigh. "Why couldn't you keep your nose out of my business? Come to think of it, how do you even know about that particular poison? You can't tell me some lousy cook actually knows about outdated poisons?"

I shook my head quickly, my throat tight as the woman stared at me with the same compassion as a spider for its prey. As Melanie's face grew redder, I thought I had better answer her question. "Yes, I did find the Thall-rat in your barn. I didn't go to the cops, though. No one would believe us anyway, right? We can't go to the cops without proof. So no one has to…"

"You stupid, stupid little cow." Melanie snatched my phone from me and flung it at the wall.

"Why did you kill him?" I asked, hoping to distract her. "He was marrying you."

"He was marrying my land." Melanie snarled as her finger tightened on the trigger, glaring at me with visible disdain. "He said he'd cleaned up his act. He said that he was going to help me clean up this town. He said that he was an environmentalist now. We talked for hours about new eco-cars and how to bring them to town. A Green Initiative. I thought he *understood*."

I nodded as she lowered her hands slightly, hoping that her outpouring would calm her down. "He lied," I said.

"Yes. I fell for it, too," Melanie stated in such a calm tone that the hairs on the back of my neck rose in alarm. "Him being a rising environmental-ist. Him loving me, I let it all slide. I took it all on faith. Then I saw him sneaking around and kissing Kayleen, the mail lady. I realised he wasn't as invested in the relationship as I was."

The woman slowly started to pace the room,

keeping the weapon trained on me. "So I looked around for his plans. I was going to break off the engagement and put him out of business with his own project. I was going to let him feel the price of betraying me, but I didn't find any hybrid cars or reforestation projects. When I looked at his emails, there he was chattering to some people about my land." She let out a sigh. "He was getting legal advice about how long he'd have to be married to me before he could take a share of my land upon divorce. I'd tell you to remember that, if I thought you were going to be around to take the advice to heart."

I felt a knot of dread at the woman's calm assessment.

Melanie gave a rueful smile. "He was already arranging to exploit the coal seam gas on my land. I couldn't allow him to destroy a whole ecosystem to make a profit. He was killing the planet. Then I found those old poisons in the barn. It was like a sign. Poison the man who was intending to poison the town by allowing coal seam gas. I started off with small doses. I kept hoping that maybe he would have a change of heart and transform before the wedding. And then after a while, I knew he wasn't going to change. He was just too far gone."

Melanie's eyes took on a glassy sheen as she smiled.

A wave of panic washed over me. I took a short breath and squeezed my eyes shut. The others had told me I was a witch. If only I'd learned some spells by now. I opened my eyes when Melanie screamed. In my despair, I had forgotten about the house.

"What's going on?" Melanie asked frantically. "What is this? Stop!"

The pistol was on the ground, right beside Melanie. The woman was staring around herself, paling as she shoved at an invisible barrier. "Help, somebody," she begged as she slammed her shoulder into an invisible wall, looking like a mime artist, albeit a noisy one, as she stumbled around in the middle of the room.

CHAPTER 25

I hurried next door to Camino's house and banged on the door frantically. After a few moments, the door swung open, revealing my startled neighbour.

I was likely more startled than she was. At first I thought the door had been opened by a giant koala, but then I realised it was Camino after all, dressed in an outsized grey koala onesie, and wearing giant fluffy koala slippers, each with rounded koala ears and a big black nose.

"It's Melanie, Brant McCallum's fiancée!" I said, trying not to stare. "The crazy woman just showed up at my house with a gun. She saw me looking around on her property and got spooked. She admitted everything about Brant's murder, but that was when I thought she was going to kill me," I said, gasping for air.

"Where is she now? Come inside!" Camino said, motioning for me to enter her home.

"The house has trapped her," I said, as I followed Koala Camino inside. "She's sitting in the centre of the room with her hands up like she's stuck there. Luckily, she dropped the gun and I don't think she can reach it from inside her, err, from inside whatever's happening to her."

"Hmm," Camino said. "We need to get her to confess, but this time she needs to confess to the police." She left the room momentarily and then returned with a small bottle. "This calls for a truth potion."

"How will we get her to drink it?"

"We'll cross that bridge when we come to it," Camino replied. "Will you call Ruprecht and the others? The phone's right over there," she said, pointing to an antique desk. "Numbers are in the book."

"Sure," I said. I had forgotten about land lines and their lack of access to contacts. I looked up Ruprecht's number in the book.

"Hello?"

"Oh, Ruprecht!" I screeched, more loudly than I had intended. "We have a problem. Melanie's in my house right now with a gun. She's trapped inside, and I'm over at Camino's. Camino has a truth potion."

"A truth potion, you say? For what reason?"

I slapped myself on the forehead. "Sorry! Melanie did it! She confessed to murdering Brant McCallum. Camino wants to give her the truth potion so she'll confess to the police."

"Yes, I think she has the right idea in mind. I'll get my granddaughter right away and head to your house," Ruprecht replied.

"Okay, we'll meet you there." I ended the call and then called Thyme. She picked up at once.

"Thyme? Can you come over right now? Melanie was watching us when we were looking through that broken down barn. She showed up with a gun, but the house trapped her inside," I said without drawing breath. "Camino's going to give her a truth potion so she'll confess to the police."

"I'll be right there," Thyme replied, and the phone went silent.

I couldn't help but smile with relief. It was good to have friends who would back me up.

Camino looked up. "Let's go!" she said urgently.

By the time we were walking up my front path, Thyme's car pulled up, followed by Ruprecht and Mint. Joys of living in a small town, I suppose, with one end of town being no more than five minutes from the other.

With that, we entered the house and turned left into the living room. I saw that Melanie hadn't moved an inch. "Get me out of here!" she yelled, waving her arms around in the air.

"Out of where?" Thyme asked, garnering a look of disapproval from Ruprecht.

"This room or whatever it is! What are you crazy people doing to me? Help! Help!" she yelled, still holding her arms up and slapping at the invisible walls.

"Camino, is it ready?" Ruprecht asked.

Camino nodded and held up the small bottle in her hand.

"Good," he replied, turning to Melanie. He crouched down beside her and spoke softly. "Melanie, we need you to be calm. What is it that you're seeing?"

Melanie settled down somewhat. "What am I seeing? You don't see the huge walls that are slowly trying to crush me?" she wailed.

"I see nothing of the sort," he remarked. "But this might help," he added, extending his hand to Camino for the potion. She placed it in his hand gently. Ruprecht uncorked the bottle and looked at Melanie. "Drink this, and everything will be over."

"You think I'm going to trust you crazy people?" she yelled. "I'm not drinking anything, especially until I'm out of this torture!"

"What torture?" Thyme said. "It's all in your mind."

"Don't tell me what I can see!" the woman snapped angrily.

Just then, I had an idea. "Even though you came here to harm me, we're not here to hurt you," I said in a calm tone, although my heart was racing. "Let us help. You seem to be hallucinating, and from what I know, that's a common occurrence when someone is exposed to too much thallium. This is the antidote. The walls will go away if you drink it."

Melanie looked down and sighed. After several moments, she glanced back up at me and nodded. "Exposure to thallium? I'll be free if I trust you and drink that?"

"You'll be free from this room, yes," I replied, careful not to make any false promises. I knew that the police wouldn't allow Melanie to be free in any true sense of the word.

Ruprecht sat patiently in his crouched position, with the potion still extended to the woman. She seemed to be thinking about her options, but as they had run out, she finally took the bottle from his hand and gulped it down.

Camino turned to Thyme and whispered in her ear. "Give it a few minutes to work before you call the police, please."

"Sure thing," she replied.

Ruprecht took the empty bottle from the woman when she had finished it, and stood back up. "It shouldn't take long to kick in," he said to us. "Then we can call the authorities."

Melanie stood up, a look of disgust on her face. "You're calling the cops?"

"Of course we are. What else would we do with a murderer?" Camino asked her.

"Are you serious?" the woman said. "Just because I killed my fiancé and then tried to kill Amelia, you're going to label me like that?" As the words left her lips, Melanie's face contorted into a sour look, like she had tasted a dozen lemons all at once. "Why did I say that? What is going on?" she asked, a look of horror draining the colour from her face.

"Perhaps your guilty conscience is finally catching up with you," Thyme said.

"So, now what?" I asked Ruprecht.

"Now, we just wait," he said. "Thyme, you can call the police now."

Melanie was still watching the others, but as the realization that she was caught kicked in, she seemed to give up. She collapsed back to the ground and sighed. "I was only doing what was best for the environment," she whispered.

At that moment, there was a loud knock on the front door and Ruprecht went to answer it. He returned with Sergeant Greer and a still-smiling Constable Stevens.

"How did you get here so soon?" I asked them. "Thyme was calling you right now."

"Alder Vervain called us," Sergeant Greer said. "He said a woman went into your house with a gun."

I saw Camino and Mint give each other a significant look, and then they both fixed me with a hard stare. I tried to look blank. "Well, good that you got here so fast," I said to the cops. I did not want the others to know that I had met Alder Vervain. They sure were acting weird about that man. I'd have to find out why. Actually, I'd like to know how Alder Vervain saw Melanie enter my house. Was he watching my house? And if so, why?

The police officers wasted no time talking to Melanie. "My name is Sergeant Greer and this is Constable Stevens. I have been told that you have something you'd like to confess. Is this true?"

Melanie slowly pulled herself up from the ground, and looked at the officer intently. "Well, of course I don't want to confess," she replied.

I shot Camino a quick glance, but she just winked at me. "What did you do to Brant McCallum?" Camino asked her.

"I killed the smug jerk, but he deserved it!" she said, the anger rising in her voice.

Both the police officers immediately gasped. "Are you admitting to your fiancé's murder?"

"It sure seems like that's what I'm doing, doesn't it?" she said, shaking her head emphatically.

Greer and Stevens exchanged glances. "You are not obliged to say or do anything unless you wish to do so, but whatever you say or do may be used in evidence. Do you understand?" he asked Melanie.

"I understand," she snapped, clamping her hand over her mouth.

Greer pulled a small notepad from his pocket and began scribbling in it. "Can you explain to me what you did to Brant McCallum, please?"

"When I found out that he was using me and seeing another woman, I lost it. I began poisoning him with small amounts of Thall-rat. It's a type of rat poison that contains thallium," Melanie said, no emotion or remorse apparent in her voice. "It was banned in Australia in the 1950s, but I found some in my old barn. I read that one gram mixed in food would kill in two weeks. The symptoms look like many other diseases, so it's hard to detect."

The two police officers looked at each other and nodded. Stevens was still smiling widely.

"Well, that sure does match up to what the evidence suggests happened, but why are you confessing to this now?" Sergeant Greer asked.

"I didn't want to!" she screamed. "The only reason I came here was because Amelia Spelled found out about the old rat poison and was going to turn me in. I saw her out at my land today. I tried to kill her, but then the walls started closing in around me! The house trapped me! I didn't want to confess, but I had to!"

Sergeant Greer couldn't resist sniggering, despite his apparent best efforts. "Excuse me? The house trapped you here and made you confess?" he asked, clearly in disbelief.

Melanie looked around the room with terror in her eyes. "Yes, that's exactly what happened!"

CHAPTER 26

I couldn't believe my ears. "What did you say to me?" I asked, placing my hands on my hip. I was standing behind the counter, facing Thyme. A line was forming behind the counter.

"You heard me, lady," Thyme said, not backing down.

I took a step forward. "Did you tell your boss that she isn't allowed in the kitchen?"

"I did," Thyme said in mock firmness. She turned and reached into the case beside me, selecting a cupcake for the next customer in line. She boxed it up and handed it over, while I took an offered credit card and ran it through the machine.

"Well, we're out of double chocolate," I went on. "And we both know you're faster out here, so let me have a go at the baking. I think by now I can get the hang of it."

"You would think so," Thyme said, chuckling, "but we can't risk setting the place on fire, as much as you'd like to see Craig."

I smiled in response. Did I want to see Craig? Well, yes, I supposed I did. Still, I couldn't get Alder Vervain out of my mind. Logically, I figured I was only attracted to Alder as he was mysterious, whereas Craig was sweet and dependable.

"I haven't set out all the ingredients," Thyme said, concern apparent in her voice.

"Oh, please, I don't need you to hold my hand any more."

Thyme pouted. "No, I need to hold you down and chain you up out here."

I waved her off. "You help the customers. I'll whip up a batch of double chocolate."

"You know, the only reason I'm letting you do this is because you're the boss," Thyme said, shaking her head.

I laughed again and went into the back. It was amazing how different I could feel in just a few days. Melanie had been arrested, and the news that she had poisoned her fiancée had spread around town pretty quickly. Business was booming. Nothing bad had been in the cakes, and now everyone knew it, and it was as if the townspeople felt so bad for avoiding the place that they were now coming in droves. There had been a lot of handshakes, a lot of smiles, and I was getting to know many of the locals rather well, even in such a short time.

My best customers were the people who owned the shops nearby. They came in for snacks throughout the day, and chatted and gossiped with me. It made me finally feel like one of them.

When I had first moved to town, I hadn't known what to expect. And to be sure, there was no way I could have known I was going to get caught up in a murder mystery, or that I would be one big reason that a killer confessed and was arrested. There had been moments of sheer terror, that was for sure, but there had also been moments of belonging, moments of friendship like I had never known.

As I selected the bowls I needed, pulling them down from a shelf bolted to the wall above the workspace, I thought of the people I had met in Bayberry Creek. Thyme was absolutely the best friend I'd ever had. Coming into work, no matter how stressful it had been for a while there, when we had no customers and the money was running out, had still been a pleasure. Thyme had been friendly and caring, and had made the move and the new responsibilities so easy on me.

And of course, she had started me down a magical path. I still couldn't quite believe that I was actually a witch. My aunt had been a witch. I lived in a temperamental house which could grow smaller or bigger, rearranging its rooms at will.

As I set out the ingredients, I thought of Ruprecht, so helpful and kind, and his granddaughter, Mint. Camino, my neighbour, was as thoughtful and caring as the others. So many people had been willing to help me out, solely because of my aunt. That was something special to me.

I had the dry ingredients in the bowl, and I used a wooden spoon to mix them, before cracking three eggs into the bowl. So far so good. If only Thyme could see me now!

The mixing went well, better than I had expected. As much bravado as I pretended to have, the idea of baking unsupervised still frightened me. Let's face it—I was a terrible cook, after all.

Nevertheless, I was doing it. Maybe I had learned something after all. It was possible, wasn't it? If someone did something long enough, even if they were terrible at it, surely they could learn to do it. Not everyone who picked up a guitar was a virtuoso when they plucked their first string. Not every writer could use words to describe a scene or a character beautifully. They learned. I could learn.

I poured the batter into cupcake tins and slid them into a preheated oven. Now I had to wait. I set the timer and went back out to the show room. There was still a line, stretching to the door. Thyme looked at me in surprise.

"Well, I guess that was better than I expected, huh?" she asked. "I can't smell smoke."

I laughed and rolled my eyes. "I told you I would be fine," I said. "No fires at all."

I settled in next to Thyme, the two of us falling into an easy rhythm. Thyme would take orders and box the cupcakes, while I took payment. A woman came in looking for a cake for her son's birthday party in a week, and Thyme broke away, taking her to the end of the counter to get her order, while I was left to handle the customers by myself. When Thyme returned, tucking the order form into an envelope by the phone on the counter, the line had died down. There was a ding from the oven out the back.

"I can get them," Thyme said, but I reached out and pressed my fingers to her arm.

"No, I got them," I said. "I want to see these through."

Thyme smiled and nodded. "Promise me there's no love potion in this batch, though."

"I only add love potion to the red velvet cake icing," I said with a laugh, hurrying through the swinging double door and into the back room.

I turned off the oven and pulled down the door, half expecting to see a horribly burnt pan with rock hard cupcakes charred black. But no, these looked good. What a shock!

I pulled out the two tins and set them on top of the oven. I then checked the bucket of cream cheese icing in a refrigerator against the wall. It would be a while before the cupcakes were cool enough to ice.

I tried to remember the last time I had been so happy. I almost felt like a kid again, in a way. That's how happy I was.

I had to turn out the cupcakes onto the cooling rack. Surely they'd had enough time to settle. I reached for one, and just before my fingers touched it, it gave off a hiss, and blew up in my face. And then, as if spurred on by the first, the others did as well. Chocolate was everywhere, on me, on the wall, the ceiling, the floor. I didn't know what I had done.

Too much baking soda? Too much flour? What could even make a cupcake blow up like that? Had they heated and cooled too fast? I had no idea.

Luckily, there were no customers in the shop when I stepped through the double doors. Thyme took one look at me, all covered in chocolate, and burst into laughter. She doubled over, unable to say anything for a long while, tears falling from her eyes. I joined her, laughing as well. Chocolate dripped down to the top of my eyelashes, and then fell onto the floor.

After a while Thyme walked to the double doors and pushed one open. She let it shut and turned around. She simply nodded, and then laughed again and shook her head. "I have to tell you, boss," she said, "and let me assure you, I'm not lying when I say this, but that's a new one for me."

I nodded. "You forgot the best part, though," I said with a laugh.

"What's that?" Thyme asked me.

"I'm the boss. I get to tell you to clean it up."

I watched the smile disappear from Thyme's face. Her mouth dropped open, and she shook her head. And then both of us fell into helpless laughter once more.

Dizzy Spells

Amelia's spells have improved, but her baking has not. She needs to make enough dough to save her crumbling cake store business. Yet that is soon the least of her worries, when a body is found on her porch and her new friend, Dianne, becomes the main suspect.

As Amelia tries to clear Dianne's name, she finds that some people in her life are not what they seem. Craig finally whisks Amelia away on a date, but Amelia's house has something to say about the matter, much to her distress.

The police say that solving the murder will be a piece of cake, but are they keeping her on a knead-to-know basis?

Will Amelia discover why Alder Vervain has been watching her?

Will she rise to the occasion and solve the murder, or will she become the next victim?

ABOUT MORGANA BEST

Best selling Aussie author, Morgana Best, grew up leaving Tim Tams for the fairies at the bottom of her garden. Now she lives with a half-blind Chocolate Labrador who happily walks into doors, a rescue Dingo who steals zucchinis from the veggie patch, and a cat with no time for nonsense. A former college professor, Morgana enjoys big bowls of pasta, not working out, and visiting the local lighthouse, where she tries to spot the white humpback whale.

www.morganabest.com

33502812R00160

Printed in Great Britain
by Amazon